"Quiet!" Benjy shouted. "Look, this man can't be the Gunsmith. Rufus King killed him."

The man to Benjy's immediate right—the other man from the saloon—said, "He's standing there ready to draw on eight armed men, Benjy. Who would *you* say he is?"

"He hasn't said a word," Benjy said. "It's this chink who's doing all the talking. Hey, China-man!" he said, directing himself to Dan. "What are you gonna be doing while your friend is trying to outdraw eight men?"

That was a question the answer to which Clint Adams was also very interested in hearing . . .

Don't miss any of the lusty, hard-riding action in the Charter Western series, THE GUNSMITH:

And coming next month:

THE GUNSMITH

31

Trouble Rides a Fast Horse

J.R. ROBERTS

CHARTER BOOKS, NEW YORK

THE GUNSMITH #31: TROUBLE RIDES A FAST HORSE

A Charter Book/published by arrangement with the author

PRINTING HISTORY
Charter Original/August 1984

ISBN: 0-441-30904-6

Charter Books are published by The Berkley Publishing Group,
200 Madison Avenue, New York, N.Y. 10016.
PRINTED IN THE UNITED STATES OF AMERICA

Dedication
To

James Garner & Jack Kelly (*Maverick*)
Clint Walker (*Cheyenne*)
James Arness (*Gunsmoke*)
Stuart Whitman (*Cimarron Strip*)
Ben Murphy, Peter Duel and Roger Davis
(*Alias Smith and Jones*)
James Stacy (*Lancer*)

ONE

As long as he lived Clint Adams would always remember that sound. The bullet struck with such impact that he could feel the vibrations in his legs.

Without thinking he pulled his rifle free and launched himself from the saddle, then hit the ground hard and rolled his way to cover. Lying on his back behind a cluster of rocks he waited for further shots and hoped that Duke had gotten out of the line of fire. The big horse usually knew what to do in situations like this. God knew they'd been through enough of them together.

The thing that surprised the Gunsmith as he lay there was that he couldn't find where he'd been hit though he was sure he'd felt the impact of the bullet. He'd been shot before, and he knew there were times when a man just couldn't feel the pain right away, but this was different. It wasn't just that he didn't feel any pain—he couldn't find a wound anywhere.

Rolling over on his belly he peered up from his cover cautiously, prepared to duck right away if a shot was coming. When there was no shot, he got to his knees, still prepared to get back under cover if the need arose. When it didn't happen it became apparent that his adversary had been either a nervous amateur, or an overconfident pro who assumed that he'd need only one shot. When the Gunsmith had leapt from the saddle, it must have seemed as if the bullet had *taken* him from it. Whatever the reason, there were no other shots, and Clint stood up and stepped out from behind the rocks.

That was when he saw Duke, standing only a few feet from where they had been when the shot came. Why hadn't the big horse moved out of range?

"Duke, boy," Clint said, moving towards the horse. "What are you doing, buddy? You're supposed to move out of the line of fire."

Clint approached the horse and put his hand on Duke's neck. He was surprised to find the animal's neck slick with sweat.

"What's the matter, boy?" he asked with concern. "We haven't ridden that far, or that hard. Let me see your eyes."

He turned Duke's head so that he could look at his eyes and didn't like what he saw. They were glassy and out of focus, as if the horse had a fever or something.

"Oh, Christ," he whispered. "Duke . . . easy boy, easy now . . ."

Backing up, he began to inspect Duke's side, and found what he was afraid he would. If the bullet had been half an inch to the right it would have hit the saddle, but as it was Duke was bleeding from a bullet hole in his side, and the saddle blanket was soaking up the blood, which was why it hadn't been immediately noticeable. Now that he'd found the hole, the blood started to drip down the animal's heaving side to the ground.

"Easy, Duke," Clint said, moving back to the big horse's neck. "Easy," he repeated, patting his best friend's neck. It was amazing to him that Duke was able to remain standing. It was no wonder Clint had felt the shot in his legs; it had missed him by a hair. But the question now was how serious the wound was, and how to get Duke some help.

"I know you can stand, big boy," Clint said, "but we've got to see if you can walk."

Almost totally forgetting about his own safety—except for that sixth sense he'd developed over the years—the Gunsmith moved out in front of his horse and took hold of the reins.

"Duke," he said, staring into the animal's glazed eyes, "come on, big boy. Take a step."

For a moment the horse didn't move, but then his incredible courage took over. Clint watched hopefully as the horse took a step forward, then another, and then a third. He was ready to let go a sigh of relief when suddenly Duke stopped, staggered a step to the right, went to his knees, and then keeled over onto his side.

"Duke," Clint said as the big horse's glassy eyes closed, and a breath sounding menacingly like his last came forth from his nostrils.

"No," Clint said in an agonizing whisper as he fell to his knees next to his friend. "Oh, no."

During all the years they had been ducking bullets together Duke had never come near anything more serious than a scratch. There were times when the big gelding carried a wounded, bleeding Clint Adams hundreds of miles, getting him help in time to save his life. Now Clint put his hand to the horse's muzzle and he could barely feel his breathing.

"Just hold on, Duke," Clint said, patting the fallen horse's neck. "Just hold on, it's time for me to return the favor."

If he had been able to throw Duke over his shoulder and carry him to town he would have, but since that wasn't possible he did the next best thing.

Using water from his canteen he poured some onto the ground, mixed it around, then scooped up a couple of handfuls of mud and packed Duke's wound with it. Hoping that this would at least slow the bleeding down, he then stood up and started running towards the nearest town.

TWO

The Gunsmith had come to the town of Scarlet, New Mexico at the request of a friend who had a ranch just outside of town.

Frank Wilcoxin was a wealthy rancher whose hobby was collecting guns, old and new. He'd needed Clint Adams to advise him in the purchase of a collection of sixteenth- and seventeenth-century handguns, and had been willing to pay the Gunsmith's way. Clint had received his friend's telegram while in Labyrinth, Texas and had immediately left for Scarlet with Duke, leaving his gunsmithing rig and team behind. He had stayed at the Wilcoxin ranch for a week, authenticated the collection for him, and saved him a pretty penny by advising him to wait for the price to come down, as he felt it would; and it did.

He had been heading back to Texas when Duke was wounded, and the town he was closest to now was Santa Dominique.

When Clint reached Santa Dominique he headed directly for the office marked "Don McGregor, Sheriff." When he burst through the door he was a bedraggled remnant of the Clint Adams of a hour earlier.

5

''What the hell—'' the sheriff demanded, missing the cup he was pouring his coffee into in surprise.

''Sheriff—'' Clint started, but no words would come after that and it took him a few moments to catch enough of his breath to try it again.

''Mister,'' the sheriff began, ''what the—'' but Clint waved him off because he felt ready to speak.

''Sheriff, my name is Clint Adams,'' he said breathlessly. ''Does that mean anything to you?''

For a moment—and for once in his life—Clint was afraid that it wasn't going to mean anything to him, but a look of recognition came over the lawman's face and he put his coffeepot and cup down.

''Well, I'll be damned if it don't,'' the man said. ''You're the one they call the Gunsmith.'' The sheriff, a tall man nearing fifty, had never been this close to anyone famous. For a moment he was excited, but then his lawman's suspicious mind took over and he frowned.

''What are you doing in my town, Mr. Adams?'' he asked. He was lawman enough to want to ask the question, but was still careful enough not to insult the Gunsmith by not calling him ''mister.''

''I need help, Sheriff,'' Clint said.

''*You* need help?'' the lawman asked, surprised. Everything he'd ever heard about the Gunsmith indicated that the man never needed anyone's help. ''What's the problem, Mr. Adams?''

Clint quickly outlined the situation for the sheriff, who listened intently.

''This horse,'' the sheriff asked when Clint was finished. ''Would that be this big black gelding I always heard about you riding?''

''Yeah,'' Clint said, ''that's him.''

The sheriff came around his desk and said, "You come with me, Mr. Adams."

"Where?"

"This is a small town, but we got a real good vet here," the sheriff said. "If anyone can help that horse of yours, he can."

Following the lawman out of the office Clint couldn't help but think, *Yeah, if he isn't already dead.*

THREE

The vet in Santa Dominique was a young man named James Burns. Clint was concerned because the man looked barely old enough to shave, but as it turned out he was a damned good vet.

Burns was a bit reluctant to go riding out of town to care for a horse who'd been shot more than an hour before, but with both the sheriff and Clint urging him on, he finally agreed. When he laid eyes on Duke, he was glad he had.

"That is the most beautiful animal I've ever seen," the man said.

"Is he alive?" the sheriff asked.

"He's got to be," Clint said, going down on one knee. "Doc, what do you think?"

"Let me have a look," the vet said, moving Clint out of the way. The Gunsmith moved around so that he was kneeling at Duke's head while the doctor examined the wound.

"This animal is amazing," the doctor said. "The mere fact that he's still alive . . ." Burns shook his head in admiration.

"Can you keep him that way?" Clint asked anxiously.

Burns looked at the Gunsmith and said sadly, "I seriously

doubt it, Mr. Adams,'' and then before Clint could respond he added, ''But I'm sure going to give it my best damn shot.''

Burns removed his jacket and then said to the sheriff, ''Mac, I'm going to need your help on this.''

''What can I do?'' the lawman asked.

''Go back to town to the general store and ask Peter Sellers if he's got any tents, or anything that can be used to make a tent.''

''A tent?'' Sheriff McGregor asked. ''Jim, what in blazes do you want with—''

''Just go and get it, will you? And bring me plenty of clean muslin and some water. You'll need a buckboard to carry all of this,'' he added, then proceeded to give the sheriff further instructions. ''Now get going.''

''Sure, sure,'' McGregor said. He looked at Clint Adams and said, ''I tol' you he was something, didn't I?''

''Git!'' Jim Burns shouted, and the sheriff got.

''What are you going to do?'' Clint asked.

Burns was probing through the mud pack that Clint had applied and said, ''You know, you may have saved this animal's life by doing this. What gave you the idea?''

''I don't know,'' Clint said, shrugging. ''I guess I remembered hearing it from someone. It was all I could think to do.''

''This animal means a lot to you, doesn't he?'' Burns asked.

''Yes, he does,'' Clint said.

''You asked me what I was going to do,'' Burns said, rolling up his sleeves. ''Well, Mr. Adams, I'm going to try and perform a miracle. I'm going to try and keep this brave, beautiful animal alive.''

''How?''

''I don't know,'' the vet said, ''but we're already ahead of the game.''

"Why?" Clint asked again.

"This wound would have killed a normal horse," Burns said. "There's no doubt in my mind, therefore, that we are dealing with an extraordinary animal. That, Mr. Adams, puts us ahead of the game."

As time went by it became obvious what the vet had in mind when he sent the sheriff to town for supplies.

Duke's size was working against him. He was so huge that the vet did not want to risk attempting to move him into town. It could have been done with several horses and some sort of traverse, but getting Duke onto the traverse and then into town would have killed him. Therefore what Burns did was erect a tent around the wounded horse to protect him from the elements, and then proceeded to try and work his miracle.

The first thing Burns did was remove the bullet, then he drained the wound and cauterized it. There were other steps, but after Clint had asked a question or two, the vet asked him what he wanted, a live horse or an education. Clint decided he wanted a live horse and remained silent thereafter.

"You know," Burns said at one point, in the middle of the night, "you're very lucky you got me instead of an old-fashioned vet, set in his staid ways."

"Really?" Clint asked, keeping his eyes on Duke while they spoke.

"I chose Santa Dominique to practice in because it was what I was looking for. A small town with no vet, a place where I could try out new techniques, and the people wouldn't complain because I was the only vet around."

"The sheriff seems to think highly of you," Clint said.

"He was one of my first patients—or rather, his dog was. His mutt had broken both front legs by jumping off the roof of the sheriff's house, and I set those legs and nursemaided the dog back to health."

"After two broken legs?"

"Remarkable, isn't it?" Burns asked, happily. "That dog runs and jumps now with just the hint of a limp."

"Not off the roof, I hope."

"I think Tiger has learned his lesson on that count," Burns said.

"I want to thank you for what you're doing here, Doc," Clint said then.

"This animal deserves the best care he can get," Burns said, "and that's all I'm trying to give him."

"Just the same, thanks," Clint said.

"Wait till you get my bill," Burns said, grinning.

"I'll pay it," Clint assured him. "I don't care how much it is."

"I just ask one favor," Burns said.

"What's that?"

"Have someone else hold your gun when I hand it to you."

During the next couple of weeks both Clint and Burns spent most of their time in that tent with Duke. There were occasions when Burns was called away, but he was never away for long.

"This is my number one patient, Clint," he told the Gunsmith. "I'll never be away from him long."

At one point Clint asked, "How long before he can get to his feet, Jim?"

"I think we'll see if he can stand up tomorrow."

"Will you walk him back to town?"

Burns shook his head.

"What are you going to do, then, put him on a traverse? You can't get him into a wagon."

"Yes, we can," Burns said. "I'm having that taken care of. The blacksmith and a carpenter from town are working on a wagon, lowering the floor so we can walk him in. It's done back East with race horses.''

"Well, I'll be damned," Clint said.

"If he can stand he'll only have to do it long enough to get back to town, then we'll lie him down again. After that, we'll let him up a little longer every day. Do you want him to convalesce in town?''

"Will he be able to travel?" Clint asked.

"Not on foot."

"I mean by train."

"Sure, I suppose so," Burns said. "Why?"

"I've got some friends in a town called Labyrinth, Texas who'll look after him for me.''

"Look after him?" Burns asked. "What are you going to be doing?''

Clint looked at Burns and said, "I'm going after the man who shot him.''

"You know who it is?"

"I will."

"How?"

"Whoever it was was shooting at me," Clint explained, "and I'd bet that he thinks he killed me.''

"So?"

"I've got Mac sending out telegrams for me," Clint went on. "Sooner or later the man who thinks he's killed the Gunsmith has got to start bragging about it, and when he does I'll get him.''

"You know," Burns said, "you're not at all what I expected the Gunsmith to be like.''

"You've heard of me?"

"Well, of course," Burns said. "Why does that surprise you?''

"Well, since we've met you never gave any indication of knowing who I was.''

"I've been a little preoccupied," Burns explained. "I read about you back East."

"Newspapers?"

"Newspapers, dime novels—"

"Dime novels?" Clint asked. "I haven't seen any of those."

"Nobody out here would have any reason to read those, would they?" Burns asked. "Strictly for the easterners, that's what I thought."

"Maybe you're right."

"Anyway, what I'm getting at is this," Burns said. "You're not what I expected a man of your reputation to be. What will you do when you find this man? Will you kill him?"

"To tell you the truth, Jim, I haven't really thought about what I'll do when I find him," Clint answered. "All I've thought about is finding him."

"Well, while you're out looking for him I don't want you to have to worry about Duke," Burns said, "and I've never seen Labyrinth, Texas."

Clint stared at the young vet and said, "You'd go to Texas with him?"

"I told you," Burns said. "He's my number one patient."

"Jim, I really appreciate this."

"Well," the younger man said, laying a hand on Duke's neck, "he's special, you know. He's come to mean a great deal to me, even as more than a patient."

"I know what you mean," Clint said.

"You do?"

"Sure," Clint said. "He's your first real miracle."

Clint had intentions of telegraphing Labyrinth and having his friend Rick Hartman either come himself or send someone to accompany Duke on the trip to Texas. Now that Jim

Burns had offered—insisted, in fact—on doing so, that was no longer necessary. He did, however, send a telegram telling Rick to expect Duke and Burns.

A few days later Duke was fairly steady on his feet, but he had lost a huge amount of weight and was only a shadow of what he had been. His coat was dull, and his ribs showed. In addition, he seemed barely able to hold his head up.

Still, it was damned good to see him back on his feet.

About two hundred miles of Union Pacific railroad track crossed the northeastern corner of New Mexico as it went from Texas to Colorado. It was there Burns would catch the train and take Duke back to Labyrinth, which had more or less become a base of operations for the Gunsmith in recent years.

"Where will you go from here?" Burns asked, the night before they were all to leave Santa Dominique.

"Wyoming," Clint said without hesitation.

"Wyoming?" Burns asked. "Have you heard something—"

"No, not yet," Clint said, "but when I do hear something I want to have a good horse beneath me, and the best horse that can be had is in Wyoming."

"One as good as Duke?" Burns asked.

"There aren't any as good as Duke," Clint said, "but this one comes damned close, Jim. A big white named Lancelot."*

"Named after Sir Lancelot?" Burns asked. "His owner must be educated."

"She is," Clint said, "and she's beautiful. Her name is Beverly Press, and she has a big spread up there. I've already sent her a telegram, and since I'm the only man who's ever

---

* The Gunsmith #28: The Panhandle Search.

ridden the horse—the only man he's ever allowed to ride him—since the death of her husband, it was a forgone conclusion that she would say yes to my request to borrow him.''

"And then where will you go from there?''

"I'll stay put until I hear something,'' Clint said.

"Do you think the widow Press will grant you that favor?'' Burns asked with a sly look.

Clint grinned at the younger man and said, "My boy, I think she'll insist on it.''

FOUR

Beverly Press not only insisted that Clint Adams stay put, but offered extra incentive to make sure he did.

The widow Press was a tall, handsome woman with a full, womanly body that Clint knew very well. Her breasts were large and heavy, tipped with large, dusky colored nipples. Her legs were long and shapely, with just a hint of extra flesh in her thighs. That extra flesh, however, made it very comfortable for a man to settle between them, as the Gunsmith was now doing.

"Mmmm," Beverly Press moaned as Clint's tongue found her love button and began circling it. "Oh, God, Clint, yes, that's it, now suck on it, please . . ."

He took the little nub between his lips and sucked on it until she was holding him behind the head, grinding her pelvis into his face. Suddenly, she grabbed him by the hair and called, "You better come right up here and stuff it in me, mister!"

"Glad to oblige," he said.

"Oh Christ," she almost yelled as he entered her, "it's been a long time between visits!"

Suddenly her body heaved up, lifting both of them off the bed with incredible strength for a woman, and then she fell

16

back and ground her bottom into the mattress while Clint exploded inside of her.

"I think I'm insulted," she said later, as they lay in bed together, regaining their breath.

"About what?"

She turned her head on the pillow so she could look at him and answered, "You only come and see me when something happens to your horse."

"That's—" he began, wanting to say it wasn't true, but it was.

"I'm teasing," she said, placing her hand on his belly and tangling her fingers in his pubic hair. "How is Duke?"

"That young vet did wonders with him, Beverly," Clint said. "I never thought I'd see ol' Duke back on his feet, but there he was, and it really was like a miracle. He's lost a lot of weight, though. He doesn't look the same."

Beverly Press heard the anguish in Clint's voice and asked, "Will he ever be the same, Clint?"

"I asked Doc Burns that question myself," he said, "just before leaving."

"What was his answer?"

Clint smiled wryly and said, "He may be a new kind of animal doctor, but he gave me an old doctor's answer."

" 'Wait and see,' " Beverly Press said, and the Gunsmith nodded.

"That and 'only time will tell,' " he added.

"It's maddening when they tell you things like that," she said, "but then I think that's why they do it."

"I suppose so," he said.

She saw the worry on his face for his beloved horse, and she sought to take his mind off of it. "Would you like to go out to the barn to see Lance?" she asked.

"Now?"

"Why not?" she said. "We can always come back here after."

He smiled at her and said, "All right."

In the barn Lance was waiting for them in the special enclosed stall Beverly's husband had built for him. It bothered Clint to see the horse in there. It was like putting him in a box.

Clint opened the stall door himself and stood staring at the magnificent white stallion. The animal was even more breathtaking than Clint remembered, but seeing him also reminded Clint of how even the stallion paled beside Duke when they were standing side by side.

It had surprised Clint that the two animals had been able to stand near each other without either issuing a challenge, but it had also pleased him. Duke did not get along with many horses, and this only spoke more in Lancelot's favor.

The main differences in the two animals were in Duke's superior size and strength, but Lancelot had an advantage in stamina as he was a few years younger. Also, Duke was a gelding and Lance was not—although whose favor that was in remained unclear.

"Hello, boy," Clint said, holding his hand out but not moving forward. He did not want to approach the horse until he was sure he remembered him.

"Come on, big fella," he called, "don't you remember me?"

Lancelot stared at Clint for several moments before seeming to nod his big head and then coming forward to nuzzle the man's hand.

"He remembers," Beverly said behind him.

"Of course he does," Clint said, patting the animal's nose.

Clint talked to the horse for about fifteen minutes or so, patting his neck and just re-establishing the rapport they'd had months before.

"All right, boy," Clint said finally, "it's time to say good night. In the morning we'll go for a ride, what do you say?"

The horse whinnied at that and seemed to be nodding his head.

"I think he really understands you," Beverly said as Clint closed the stall door.

"Tomorrow I want to take him out of this stall and keep him out until it's time for us to leave."

"That's fine, since you're here to handle him," she said. "I've got a couple of men who are minus fingers because of him."

Clint frowned, fearful for the horse, and asked, "Is it wise to keep such men on?"

She laughed and said, "They're horsemen, Clint. They don't hold a couple of fingers against such a magnificent animal."

"Glad to hear it," Clint said, taking her by the elbow and steering her towards the barn door.

"Where are you leading me to, sir?" she asked.

"Back to the warmth of your bed, madam," he replied. "We've got a lot of catching up to do."

FIVE

For the next few days Clint took Lancelot out several times, just so they could familiarize themselves with each other. However, other than riding Lance by day and Beverly Press by night, there wasn't much for him to do while waiting for a telegram from either McGregor, or somewhere else, telling him where to start looking for the man who tried to kill him and very nearly succeeded in killing Duke.

In addition, there was the fact that Meade, the foreman, and he did not get along. He knew that before he had come along a few months ago, it had been Meade who warmed Beverly's bed when her need arose, and he did not know if they had gone back to that arrangement in his absence. During the day, when he was either riding Lance or simply walking around, he could feel Meade's eyes on him, waiting for him to drop dead from natural causes. The one thing he figured he didn't have to fear was that Meade would try to hurry that moment along. The man didn't like him, but he was no killer.

"Has Meade given you any trouble?" Beverly asked him one night in bed.

"Not really," Clint said. "If looks could kill I'd be dead

several times over, but that's about it.''

"I could speak to him," she offered.

"That sure wouldn't improve relations any," Clint assured her. "Why don't we just let it alone? I don't know what your relationship is with him when I'm not around—"

"Well, there have been some cold nights since you were here last," she interjected.

"—but he'll feel a lot better when I'm gone."

"Just as long as he doesn't try anything while you're here," she said. "He knows you're my guest."

"Yeah," Clint said, "and that's what's rubbing him the wrong way."

"Well," she said, sliding her thigh over him, and then rubbing her pubic patch against his semi-erect cock, "I hope I'm not rubbing you the wrong way."

"Never," he said. He took hold of her hips, eased her onto him fully, and then probed with the swollen tip of his penis until he was inside her, taking her breath away.

"Yes," she said. First she rubbed her large breasts against his chest, enjoying the way his chest hairs scratched her nipples, and then she sat up straight, with her knees on either side of him, and bounced up and down, gasping each time his cock achieved maximum penetration. "Oh, yes, damn you!"

Everytime she came down on him he thrust his hips up to meet her, and as she increased her speed, her gasps became hoarse cries, until suddenly she stiffened and then ground her pelvis against him as they both came together.

"I'm going to be very sorry when this visit is over," she said afterward.

"Look at it this way," he said, putting his arm around her, "I've got to bring the horse back, don't I?"

● ● ●

Early the next morning, the visit came to an end. While they were busy wishing each other good morning, there was a knock at the door.

"Damn!" Beverly snapped beneath her breath—from beneath the Gunsmith. He grinned down at her as she called out, "Yes?"

"I'm sorry to bother you, Miz Press," Beverly's housegirl called out.

"What is it, Amanda?"

"There's a man at the door who says he has a telegram for Mr. Adams."

Beverly made a face, because she knew that this meant he would be leaving. "Tell him I'll be down in a couple of minutes," Beverly instructed.

"Yes, ma'am."

"That'll be the telegram you've been waiting for," she said, looking up at him sadly.

"Hopefully," he said.

"Well, you don't have to look quite so hopeful," she said, "especially considering your present location." She wiggled her hips to bring her point across.

"You're right."

"Well," she said, looking at him sternly, "let's make this a good one, then, because it may be the last for a while."

He proceeded to make it as good as he could, but he knew that although it might be their last together for a while, it certainly wouldn't be the last for either one of them.

"What is it?" Beverly asked.

Clint folded it up and put it in his pocket, and she could tell by the look on his face that it was what he'd been waiting for since his arrival five days before.

"A man named Rufus King was heard to be bragging that he'd killed Clint Adams, the Gunsmith."

"Where?" she asked.

"A little Arizona town called Muller," Clint said thoughtfully.

"Rufus King," Beverly repeated. "Do you know the name?"

"I don't know," he said, staring off at something she couldn't see. "It sounds familiar."

She gave him a few moments to think about it, and then asked, "What are you going to do now?"

"Now," he said. "Can you get that man back here, the one who brought the telegram?"

"Of course," she said. "Why?"

"I want to send a telegram."

"To Arizona?"

"To Texas," he said. "I want to check on Duke's condition before I leave."

"When do you want to leave?"

"Today," he said. "Can you have him wait for an immediate reply?"

"Yes, of course."

"I'll just write it out."

She took him to her office, and then sent for the man while he wrote out his message. Back in her office she asked Clint, "Would you like me to have Lance saddled?"

"Only if you want some of your men to lose a few more fingers," he said. He was seated behind her desk, but she didn't mind a bit. "There's plenty of time for that."

"Clint, what will you do to this man when you find him?" she asked.

"You're the second person to ask me that, Beverly," he told her, "and the answer is the same. My first objective is to find him. After that . . ."

"Would you . . . kill him, simply for shooting your horse?" she asked.

The way she said it, it sounded ridiculous to kill a man for shooting an animal.

"The man's intention was to kill me," Clint said. "That he shot my horse was accidental."

"Then would you kill him for something he did accidentally?" she asked.

"You're making this all sound wrong," he said, standing up. "Besides, I haven't said anything about killing him."

"Isn't that the only reason a man like the Gunsmith would hunt another man?" she asked.

"That's not fair," he said quickly.

"I know," she said, "and I meant it that way." She approached him and took hold of his arm. "Forget about Rufus King, Clint. Duke's all right and so are you, so why don't you just stay here a little longer and then go on about your business?"

"It would be nice to do as you suggest," he said after a moment, "but I can't."

"Why not?"

"Because that man tried to kill me," he explained, "and when he finds out I'm alive he'll try again."

"So you'll kill him first," she said, "because that's what the *Gunsmith* would do, isn't it?"

"Beverly—"

"All right," she said, cutting him off, "maybe I'm being unfair. Maybe you've got to do what you've got to do. I don't know."

He had been going to suggest that they go back upstairs, but it didn't seem appropriate now.

"I'll go out and see to Lance," he said. "You'll let me know when your man gets back?"

"Of course," she said. "It shouldn't be too long."

"Thanks," he said, "for everything, Bev."

"Sure," she said. "What are friends for?"

Later, she brought him his reply from Texas, from the vet, Jim Burns.

"Duke's getting better," she said, handing it to him. "I hope you don't mind . . . I read it."

"I don't mind," he assured her. He read it himself, then folded it and put it in the same pocket as the other one. It was brief, saying that Duke seemed to be recovering, and that he was putting on weight.

She waited while he finished saddling Lance, tying his bedroll into place and throwing his saddlebags onto his back. He picked up his Springfield, slid it into place on the saddle, then turned to face her.

"That's it, then?" she asked.

"That's it," he said. "I'm ready to go."

"Then go," she said, "and don't forget that he tried to kill you once and you're putting yourself right in his sights again."

"I won't forget." He considered for a moment embracing her, but decided against it and mounted up. "I'll see you soon, Bev."

"Sure," she said.

He rode out of the barn and guided Lance towards the road to town, which he would follow briefly.

As he rode away he suddenly heard Beverly shouting behind him.

"Just don't get my horse shot, you . . ."

SIX

Muller, Arizona was a very small town, with one hotel, one saloon, one livery stable, and no telegraph office. When Clint registered in the hotel he paid the clerk for a look at the register. King had been there, but he'd checked out during the time it had taken Clint to ride from Wyoming to Arizona.

"Did he say where he was headed?" he asked the clerk.

"No, sir," the clerk replied. Clint waved more money beneath the man's nose, and although he could have lied for it, he did not. He didn't know where King was headed, and Clint gave him the money anyway.

Next, Clint checked in with the town sheriff, a man named Parker.

"Yeah, I know who King is," the sheriff said in reply to Clint's question, "but I don't know where he was headed when he left."

"Were you the one who sent a message to Sheriff McGregor in New Mexico?"

"Yeah, that was me," Parker said. "I know Mac, and when I heard he was looking for someone bragging about killing the Gunsmith, I sent my deputy to the next town to notify him. You're the Gunsmith, huh?"

"Yeah, I'm him," Clint said.

"You got some kind of beef with King?" Parker asked. "You gonna kill him?"

"Thanks for your help, Sheriff," Clint said, turning to leave.

"Okay, so it's none of my business," Parker said. "How long you planning to stay in my town, Adams?"

"Not long."

"Just long enough to find out where King was headed when he left?"

"Not long," Clint said, again.

"Well, you might as well check the saloon," Parker suggested. King spent a lot of time there sampling the whiskey and the women upstairs. Maybe somebody there can help you."

"Much obliged, Sheriff," Clint said, and left the office.

The saloon was a small place with five tables and a small bar.

"What'll you have?" the bartender asked when Clint came in.

"Beer," Clint said.

The bartender, a corpulent man of about fifty who barely seemed to have enough room to move about behind the bar, brought the beer back and then leaned his forearms on the bar.

"You looking for some company?" the man asked.

Clint took a sip of the lukewarm beer and asked, "What did you have in mind?"

"We got some girls upstairs who get pretty lonely," the man said.

"Is that so?" Clint asked. "How many do I have to choose from?"

"Three," the man said. "Best girls in Arizona."

If that was the case, Clint wondered, what the hell were they doing in this dusthole?

"Two brunettes and a blonde," the bartender said.

"What, no redhead?"

"She left town," the man said.

"I'm looking for a friend of mine who was in town recently," Clint said. "Rufus King."

The bartender stood up straight and said, "I don't ask names, friend."

"Well, I know he was here and that he's not here anymore, but if I knew which girl he picked, I'd know which one to pick," Clint explained. "See, my friend and I have the same taste in women."

That seemed to mollify the man some and he leaned his forearms on the bar again.

"That being the case," he said, "you'll spend a lot of time with Molly."

"Would she be available right now?"

"Uh, she's busy right now, but if you want to wait," the man said, "take a table. Otherwise you can have one of the others. They're just as good."

"No," Clint said. "I think I'll wait for Molly."

He took his beer and walked to a table set against the wall. Two of the other tables were empty. At another, a man sat alone with his bottle, and at one two men were playing poker for pennies. From the look of them, Clint had the feeling that they were around to make sure no one got rough with the girls.

He soon found out that he was right.

Ten minutes later there was some commotion upstairs, and a girl came running out onto the balcony above the room. From the open door behind her came an Oriental man.

"Benjy!" she shouted. "This guy's giving me a hard time."

Benjy was apparently the bartender, and he looked over at

the two men playing poker and jerked his head. They dropped their cards and charged up the steps.

The girl backed out of their way and they approached the Oriental and grabbed him by the arms. The man offered no resistance but looked unconcerned by the whole thing.

They hustled him down the steps, and that's when he ceased to be so relaxed. "I request that you let go of me," he said.

"Is that so?" one of the men said. "Well, you was hassling one of the girls, friend, and for that you get a lesson."

The man drew back a hamlike fist to drive it into the little Oriental's stomach, and for a moment Clint considered stepping in. If he did that, however, he might blow any chance of getting information about King.

He was still undecided about what to do when the situation resolved itself.

As the man swung his fist with murderous force, suddenly the Oriental was no longer there. The first man's fist swung through thin air and, as he was off balance the Oriental shouted, "Kaii!" and kicked him in the groin. The first man went down and the second turned to see where the little man had gone, only the Oriental was on the move again. He got behind the second man and threw a kick into his kidney area, knocking him to his knees. The first man was on the floor, rolling around with his hands clasped to his groin.

"Goddamn chink!" Benjy the bartender shouted. He reached beneath the bar and came up with a Greener shotgun, but before he could pull the trigger—and before Clint could decide to move—the Oriental was suddenly in the air, flying over the bar. Clint watched in awe as the little man kicked out, catching the bartender on the butt of the jaw, and ended up standing on top of the bar while the fat man slid down behind it.

From atop the bar the Oriental turned to look up at the girl.

"I would still like to know where the man called King went," he announced to the girl.

"Go to hell in a rickshaw," the girl shouted, and ran into her room, slamming the door behind her.

The Oriental shrugged, and dropped down lightly from atop the bar. He was headed for the steps when Clint spoke up.

"Excuse me," he called.

The Oriental turned to face Clint, seeming very relaxed, but the Gunsmith knew better than to believe that.

"I am sorry if I have disturbed your repast," the small man said. "Please forgive me."

"I will if you'll have a drink with me," Clint said.

"I am sorry," the man replied, "but the young lady has some information that it is imperative I have. If you will excuse me."

"I really think you should have that drink with me," Clint said.

The man looked less relaxed now. "Why?"

"Because we're looking for the same man," Clint said.

"King?" the Oriental asked.

"That's right."

The other man took several steps towards Clint's table and said, "Why are you looking for him?"

"I think maybe we should talk about this someplace else," Clint said, "before your dance partners collect themselves again."

The Oriental looked down at the two men on the floor, who were trying to get to their feet, then whirled and kicked out again, twice, catching each of them on the side of the head.

"I'm impressed," Clint said, standing, "but I still don't think we should be seen talking together here."

Clint walked to the bar and reached over it to grab a bottle of whiskey, glancing down at the sleeping bartender as he did.

"What do you suggest?" the Oriental asked.

"Let's go find a quiet place to sit and talk," Clint said. "We just might be able to help each other."

SEVEN

Dan Chow was twenty-nine, stood about five four, and had spent much of his formative years growing up in San Francisco's Chinatown. His family—his parents, himself and his sister—came to the United States from China during the early 1850's, looking to become rich from the gold that grew on trees in California. Unfortunately, when they arrived they found that this was not exactly the way things were.

His parents died soon after, and Dan was left to care for himself and his younger sister. His real name was Chow Lo Dan, his sister's name was Chow Li Su.

"She calls herself Sue Chow," he said. "She is twenty-six now. She was but an infant when we arrived in this country, and now she is a beautiful woman."

"Where is she?"

"In San Francisco," Dan answered. "She chose to stay there when I left."

"And where did you go?"

"I traveled," Dan said.

They were in the livery stable, which was deserted but for Lance and a few other horses. The liveryman was nowhere to be found, which was just as well.

32

"I have told you about myself," Dan said. "Now you must do the same."

Briefly, Clint told Dan Chow who he was, and Dan nodded, obviously having heard of the Gunsmith.

"I have heard stories," he said. "Why is it you seek the man Rufus King?"

"He tried to kill me about a month back, almost killed my horse instead."

"This has angered you?"

Clint nodded. "I get upset when people try to kill me," he said.

"Just so," Dan said.

"Why are you looking for him?"

Dan looked down at the dirt floor and said, "He killed my wife."

"When was this?"

"Two months ago, in Montana," Dan said, "after he turned her into a whore."

"I'm sorry."

"I do not wish to talk about it," Dan Chow said. "I merely wish to find him as you do. You said that we could help each other."

"Well, it seems to me that you were having some trouble getting information out of that girl—Molly, wasn't it?"

"Yes, that was her name," Dan said. "The bartender told me that she was his best girl. I assumed, knowing Rufus King, that this was the girl he would prefer."

"Good thinking," Clint said. Dan Chow obviously knew King on sight, which meant he'd be handy to have around. "I have a suggestion. I think maybe I should go back to the saloon and act like I want to use the girl. Did you try to pass yourself off as a client?"

"No. I do not use prostitutes," he said with great vehemence.

"I don't either," Clint said, "but this is business, and not pleasure. I'll go back and hopefully none of the men you knocked out will remember that we spoke, or left together."

"What will I do?"

"Do you have a hotel room?"

"No."

"Go and stay in mine, then," Clint said. "Get some rest until I come back, and with luck I'll have some information for us to go on."

"All right," Dan Chow said, standing up. Clint stood, and Dan looked up at him. "You will not leave town without telling me?"

"My gear is in the room, Dan," Clint said. "I won't leave."

"Are you an honorable man, Clint?" Dan asked.

"I like to think so."

"What do you plan to do with Rufus King when you find him?" the Oriental asked.

Everyone was asking Clint that question lately. Maybe he should start asking himself. "I haven't decided, Dan."

"You will not kill him?"

"I don't know. I only know that I want to find him."

"When I find him I will kill him," Dan said, with feeling. He looked at Clint again and said, "If we find him together, Clint, I will kill him. If you try and stop me, or try to kill him yourself, we will fight."

Clint looked down at the smaller man and knew that the last thing he wanted to do was fight with him.

"I'll remember that, Dan," he promised.

EIGHT

As Clint entered the saloon Benjy was standing behind the bar with his head in his hands, and the other two men were back at their table, though not sitting up as straight as they had before.

Clint approached the bar and asked, "Are you all right?"

Benjy looked up at him, saw who it was and narrowed his eyes suspiciously. "And where were you?"

"What do you mean?"

"Why didn't you take a hand?"

"I never buy into another man's trouble," Clint said. "And besides, there were three of you against one. I felt so confident that I left, figuring I'd come back when the trouble was over. Why, what happened?"

Benjy frowned and said, "We gave that chink what for, that's what happened."

"Well, good for you," Clint said. "Do you think Molly would be free now?"

Benjy, touching the side of his head where it had come in contact with Dan Chow's foot, said, "I'm sure she's free."

"Then I'd like to visit her," Clint said.

"Yeah, sure," Benjy said, dropping his hand. "You'll have to pay me first—"

"I don't pay for anything in advance, friend," Clint told the fat bartender, staring him steadily in the eyes.

"I'm afraid that's the way—"

"Just tell me what room she's in, friend," Clint interrupted him, "and I'll pay you on the way out—if I'm satisfied."

"Now, look—"

"Would you pay for a meal that was inedible?" he asked, choosing an analogy that fit the man's corpulent physique.

"You've got a point," Benjy agreed. Besides, he thought, he could up the price afterward. Molly never failed to satisfy a man's needs. Benjy knew that from personal experience—he *experienced* all his girls.

"When you're satisfied, you can pay," the bartender said. "She's in room three."

"Thanks," Clint said. He turned to leave, then noticed the two men at the table and turned back. "It looks to me like those men need a drink."

"Yeah," Benjy said, "you're probably right about that."

Clint nodded, and walked to the steps. At the top he found room number three and knocked.

"Come in," a girl's voice called.

Clint entered and shut the door behind him. The girl on the bed was a blonde, full breasted and blowsy, but attractive in a slutty sort of way.

She was wearing a plain skirt and white peasant blouse which was off one shoulder so far that the nipple of one pear-shaped breast showed.

"Well, you're a handsome one," she said. She crooked a finger at him and said, "Come on over here where I can see you better."

Clint walked across the room to the bed where she was sprawled, and the pink nipple of her breast seemed to wink at him as she moved, ducking into and then out of her blouse.

When he was close to her she reached out and placed her hand over the bulge in his pants, a developing condition he had no control over.

"And you're a big one, too," she said. "Did you pay the bartender on the way up?"

"No."

She frowned, then pressed on his erect penis and said, "Wanted to look over the merchandise first, huh?"

"No," Clint said. "I told him I would pay him if I was satisfied with the service I got."

She pulled her hand back and asked, "What do you mean, *if* you're satisfied? Ain't no man ever been with me and not been satisfied."

"I'd have to judge for myself, wouldn't I?" Clint asked. "I mean, you look like you'd know what you're doing, but you can't tell what a book's going to be like by looking at the cover."

"Bah!" she said, getting to her knees on the bed. "I don't know nothing about books, but I know about what you want." Her hands went to his belt and started undoing it and she said, "Get your pants off, mister, and I'll show you satisfaction like you ain't never had."

Clint began to resist, but the girl was persistent. While he tried to keep her from undoing his pants she undid the buckle of his gunbelt, and then when he grabbed his gunbelt, she undid his belt. Soon he was standing with his gunbelt in his hand and his pants around his ankles, and the girl feverishly freed his rigid organ from his underwear and stuffed it into her mouth.

"Listen, Molly . . ." he said, but she wasn't listening. She was sucking on his penis while her tongue beat a tattoo on its underside.

Suddenly, she let him slide free and whipped her blouse over her head. Discarding it, she took hold of his penis again and placed it between her large breasts. Squeezing her breasts together she rolled his hot column of flesh between them, flicking at the tip with her tongue at the same time.

"You like this, huh?" she asked huskily, pressing her breasts together. "Yeah, I can see you like it. I can feel you coming alive between my tits. Yeah . . ." she said, laving his tip with her tongue again.

She took his penis into her mouth again and fondled his balls in her hands while she suckled him. With his gunbelt still held in one hand, he put his other hand to the back of her head and began moving his hips in time with her bobbing head.

"Mmmm," she said with him in her mouth, squeezing his balls lightly . . . and suddenly he was filling her mouth, and she was expertly accommodating all he could give her without spilling a drop.

"Mmmm," she said again, and allowed his still stiff member to slide free of her mouth, capturing an errant last drop from the tip.

"Now," she said, backing away from him with a lewd smile on her face, "tell me that didn't satisfy you."

"Actually," he said, pulling his pants back up and belting his gun on again, "it did sort of satisfy a need—but that wasn't the need I came to satisfy."

"What are you talking about?"

"I understand you spent a good deal of time with a friend of mine recently."

"Who do you mean?" she demanded, placing her hands on her hips.

"Rufus King."

"Ha," she laughed, throwing her head back. He hadn't noticed before, but her face and still naked breasts had sort of a puffy look, as if she were on her way to getting fat in a few years. "You're the second man today who's looking for

Rufus, and you won't find him either. Now you better get out of here before you get what he got—"

"Another man?" Clint asked, hoping he looked distressed. "Was he . . . Oriental?"

"He was Chinese," she said, frowning.

"You didn't tell him anything, did you?" he asked, still trying to show concern. Actually, he *was* concerned—that he might not get any information out of her.

"No, I didn't tell him any more than I told you," she said, "which is nothing. Why?"

"That's good," he went on, as if she hadn't asked a question. "Rufe has enough problems as it is."

"Rufe?"

"That Chinaman has been looking for him for months," he said. "If there was only some way I could let Rufe know that he's getting close." He turned to her and asked, "He was here not long ago, wasn't he?"

"Well, yeah . . ." she answered.

"Then that Chinaman is too close," he said, as if talking to himself. "I'll have to get moving and see if I can find Rufe, to warn him."

"You're a friend of Rufe's?" she asked.

"Oh, sure, but hey, there's no way you could know that, Molly," he said. "You're right not to tell me anything."

He turned to leave, hoping she'd stop him before he got to the door.

"Hey, mister—"

"Yeah?"

She stood there looking puzzled, her hands still on her hips, turning at the waist from left to right while she tried to make up her mind about something. He watched in fascination as her full breasts swayed back and forth.

"Maybe I can help you," she said, finally making up her mind.

"I don't want to pressure you into anything, Molly," Clint said. "If Rufus swore you to secrecy—"

"Well, see, I really don't know anything," she told him, "but I could maybe point you in the right direction."

"Really?" Clint said. "If you could do that, Molly, I might be able to find him and warn him."

"Well," she said, taking a few steps towards him, "all I can remember is that he said he had to go to Nevada to meet some partners of his."

"Nevada?"

"Yes, but he didn't mention what town."

Still, he thought, it gave him and Dan Chow a direction to go in.

"Does that help?" she asked.

"Actually," he said, "it helps quite a lot, Molly. It gives me someplace to start."

Smiling now—which actually made her face much prettier—she said, "When you find Rufe, will you tell him that I helped you out?"

"You bet, Molly," Clint said. "I'll make sure you get all the credit you deserve."

"Great," she said, happily. "And now," she added, moving close to him, pressing her naked breasts against his chest, "now that I know you're a friend of Rufe's, is there anything else I can do for you?"

"Well," he said, "now that you mention it. I am a little short of money."

She frowned at him and said, "That wasn't exactly what I had in mind. I don't have any money—"

"I don't want to borrow money," he said. "I just don't have any to give to Benjy."

"Ah, I see," she said. "Well, you could go out the window."

"Would that get you into trouble?"

"I can handle Benjy," she assured him.

"Molly, I get the feeling you can handle most any man," he said.

She put her arms around him so that she could flatten her big breasts against his chest, and reached in between them to cup one hand over his groin.

"I handle a man the way he likes to be handled, honey," she told him, kissing him on the mouth. "You sure you can't stay a while longer—on the house?"

"I'd love to stay, sweetheart," he told her, "but if I'm going to catch Rufe before that Chinaman does, I'm going to have to leave right now."

She pouted, then kissed him and tried her best to tear his tongue out by the roots, to give him something to remember her by.

"The window," he breathed when she released his mouth.

"Right this way."

She had to flick off three different locks in order to get the window open and Clint commented on that.

"Are you kidding? This place is all Benjy's got, and he's real scared that somebody's gonna steal something from him."

"Like one of his girls?"

"Yeah," she said, grinning, "like one of his girls. You say hi to Rufe for me, hear?"

"I will."

"Hey, wait, mister," she said, grabbing his arm as he started to climb through the window.

"What?" he asked, trying to control his impatience to get out of there.

"I don't even know your name," she said. "What if I see Rufe before you do?"

He studied the girl for a second, then made a carefully calculated decision in a split second. He doubted that the girl would know him if he gave her his real name, but on the off chance that she would somehow see King first, he certainly would.

"If you should see him," he said, "tell him Clint Adams was looking for him."

"Clint Adams," she repeated, and he could tell it meant nothing to her. "I'll tell him."

"Okay," he said, and started climbing through the window.

"Hey," she said, grabbing his arm again.

"What!"

"I was just wondering why that Chinaman was so all fired anxious to find Rufe?"

He studied her again, then just said, "Well, I'm not all that sure, Molly, but I think it has something to do with too much starch. Bye."

When Clint entered his hotel room he didn't immediately see Dan Chow, and thought for a moment he wasn't there. He turned up the lamp and it was not until the light flooded the whole room that he saw Dan Chow. The Oriental had been standing in the shadows, so silent that he might not have been breathing.

"I thought for a moment you weren't here," Clint said.

"The shadows are there to be used," Dan said. "You spoke to the girl."

"I did."

"What did she tell you?"

"That Rufus King was headed for Nevada when he left here," Clint said.

The Oriental frowned and asked suspiciously, "Why did she do that?"

"Don't go getting suspicious on me, Dan," Clint said.

"I convinced her that I was a friend of King's, and that I didn't want her to tell me where he went."

Dan remained silent for a few moments, and then said, "I am embarrassed."

"Why?"

"I should have thought to do that myself," he said. "Convince a woman that you do not want her to talk, and she will talk. It is simple, but brilliant."

"Well," Clint said, not knowing quite how to react, "I've had an experience or two with women before."

NINE

Dan Chow slept on the floor of Clint's room, and in the morning Clint checked out.

"Do you have a horse?" he asked Dan.

"Yes, in the livery."

"We might as well get started, then," Clint said.

"Where?" Dan asked. "You still haven't told me how you will find King."

"We'll just follow a straight line from here to there," Clint said.

"To where?"

"To wherever he is," Clint said.

"And people say Orientals speak in riddles," Dan Chow said, seriously. Clint was starting to believe that there was no humor in this man.

On the way to the livery Clint explained that although he was not an expert tracker by any means, he had hunted his share of men. Wherever Rufus King was headed, if he didn't know there was someone on his trail, he would travel in the straightest line from where he was to where he was going.

"Does he know you're after him?"

"I do not believe so," Dan Chow said. "To be perfectly honest, this is the closest I have ever come."

"And he thinks I'm dead," Clint said. "There's no reason for him to be evasive, or to cover his tracks."

"I believe I understand," Dan Chow said, "and that I have a lot to learn.

The Oriental was dressed in trail clothes, with a flat brimmed black hat, and he looked at home in them.

"Dan, do you have a gun?"

"A revolver?"

"Yes."

"In my saddlebag."

"Can you use it?"

"Quite well—but I rarely find the need to. I am able to handle most situations without it."

"Like yesterday?"

"That was a minor problem," Dan said.

"Three men?"

"They barely made up one man," Dan said.

"Maybe, but I'd appreciate it if you'd strap your gun on during this trip," Clint said. "We may run into some trouble that will be more than an arm's length—or a leg's—away."

"Very well," Dan said.

When they reached the livery they each went about the business of saddling their horses.

"Dan—" Clint started to say, but Dan Chow made a sharp chopping motion with his hand and said, "Shh."

Clint frowned, but remained silent while Dan Chow listened intently to something the Gunsmith couldn't hear.

"Seven men," Dan said finally. "Perhaps eight. One of them is very heavy."

"Where?" Clint asked, but just then he became aware of the approaching footsteps as well.

"There," Dan said, pointing to the door of the stable, and as he did the door was filled with men, led by Benjy, the bartender and procurer.

Clint and Dan faced the door, feet spread, their weight distributed to accommodate their own special talents.

The big man remained in the doorway, but the men behind him fanned out on either side of him.

"Eight," Clint said to Dan.

TEN

"You boys got some dues to pay," Benjy said. Out from behind the bar he looked even fatter. He was holding his Greener shotgun in his hands.

"But I wasn't satisfied," Clint told the bartender. "You said I didn't have to pay if I wasn't satisfied."

"No, *you* said that, mister," Benjy said. "I brought my friends with me to tell you that you do have to pay."

"And me?" Dan Chow.

"You, Chinaman," Benjy said, looking at Dan Chow, "I owe you, and two of my friends owe you, and this is one debt you're going to be sorry to collect."

Clint Adams had no illusions about himself when it came to handling his gun. He knew that if there were half as many men, he could take them with his gun, but eight was too many, especially considering the fact that, at the moment, Dan Chow was unarmed. Clint was sorry he hadn't made the man strap on his gun before they left the hotel.

"How do you want to do this, Benjy?" he asked.

"That's up to you, friend," Benjy said. "You want to go for your gun, we'll oblige you. You want to take it off, we'll go along with that, too."

It was time to make a decision. Should he draw his gun and

take a chance on killing the unarmed Dan Chow in the process or should he discard his gun and take a chance on getting beaten to death?

Before he could decide, however, the Oriental stepped in to take a hand.

"I think perhaps we will use my friend's gun," he said.

Benjy frowned at Dan and several of the other men started to laugh.

"Chinaman," Benjy said, "you can't be that dumb. Nobody can be that dumb."

"Well, I do not stand here with just any man at my side," Dan Chow said. "With such a man I would brave twice your number."

"What is he talking about?" one of the other men asked.

"Nothing," Benjy said. "He's just runnin' off at the mouth, is all."

Hooking his fingers in his belt Dan Chow announced to the eight men in general, "You gentlemen may draw your weapons whenever you are ready."

"Chinaman, you're crazy!" Benjy said.

"My friend, Clint Adams, will draw his gun in five seconds," Dan said.

"You and your friend—" Benjy began, but one of the other men spoke up and interrupted him.

"Did he say Clint Adams?" It was one of the men with whom Dan had fought in the saloon.

"Yeah. So?" Benjy said.

Another man said, "Hey, that's the Gunsmith."

"Hey . . ." a third man said.

"Take it easy," Benjy said. He was chewing his lip as he thought this new development over. It was clear to Clint that he was the key. The other men would abide by whatever decision he made.

Clint thought that his best bet right at that moment was to remain silent and see what developed.

''That's the guy Rufus King was bragging that he killed,'' one of the other men said to the man next to him.

"Quiet!" Benjy shouted. "Look, this man can't be the Gunsmith. Rufus King killed him.''

The man to Benjy's immediate right—the other man from the saloon—said, "He's standing there ready to draw on eight armed men, Benjy. Who would *you* say he is?''

"He hasn't said a word,'' Benjy said. "It's this chink who's doing all the talking. Hey, Chinaman!'' he said, directing himself to Dan. ''What are you gonna be doing while your friend is trying to outdraw eight men?''

That was a question the answer to which Clint Adams was also very interested in hearing.

"I will kill you first, fat man,'' Dan Chow said.

Benjy wanted to laugh, but something in the Chinaman's eyes wouldn't let him.

"All right then, boys,'' Clint said, finally speaking up. ''My friend and I are ready to leave. It's up to you whether we do so over you, or around you. Dan,'' he said to his partner, ''the fat man is all yours.''

With that Clint began to back towards Lance, keeping the big horse to his right, not behind him. He remembered Beverly Press's last words to him.

"All right,'' Benjy said, and he swung the Greener around. The two men who had been with him in the saloon also went for their guns.

The Gunsmith drew and fired twice before either man could clear leather, but most of the attention was on Benjy, who was slumping to the floor with a glittering metal star sticking out of his forehead.

"*Shuriken*,'' Dan said to Clint. "A razor-sharp star-shaped knife, if you will.''

Benjy was lying on his back with this *shuriken* resting between his eyes, and there was barely any blood.

The remaining five men looked down at their three dead

comrades, and then looked at each other.

"You men have a decision to make for yourselves now," Clint said. "Your decision maker is dead. What do you want to do?"

One man slid over to the door and backed out, and that made the decision for all of them. One by one they moved towards the door and fled, leaving their three dead friends behind.

Dan Chow walked over to the dead bartender, reached down and removed his *shuriken* from the man's head.

The Gunsmith holstered his gun. "I think we ought to ride right out, Dan."

"You do not wish to speak to the sheriff of this town about this incident?"

"Ordinarily, I would," Clint said, "but in this case it would only delay us. I also don't want word that I'm still alive to reach King."

"The others . . . ?" Dan said, mounting his horse.

"I think these were the main three," Clint said, swinging atop Lance. "I don't think the others know how or where to reach King. If we leave now, we've got a better chance of catching up to him. What do you say?"

Dan looked at Clint and nodded. "I am guided by you in these matters, Clint. I believe that you are a man of honor, and would not ask me to do something that would compromise mine."

"I'm touched by your confidence," Clint said.

They rode out of the livery—literally stepping over the body of Benjy—and immediately rode out of town. Once they were about a mile out Clint called out for Dan to stop.

"What is wrong?"

"I just want to get something straight," Clint said.

"What?"

Clint pointed back to town with his thumb and said, "You

seemed to have more confidence in me than I did back there.''

''I doubt that.''

''Well, in any case, you had a lot of confidence in me. You offered to let me take care of seven of them while you took care of Benjy.''

''Oh, that was a bluff,'' Dan said.

''What?''

Dan Chow nodded and said, ''Yes, I was prepared to handle three of them.''

''Three?'' Clint asked.

The Oriental nodded. ''That is all the *shuriken* I have.''

ELEVEN

During the ride to Nevada, Dan Chow spoke very little, and when he did it was not about himself. He talked about his mother, his father—who both worked very hard to bring himself and his sister to this country to start a new life—and he talked about his sister, who was an independent woman making her way alone in San Francisco.

"Do you correspond with her at all?" Clint asked.

"We exchanged letters in the beginning," he said, "but it is hard for letters to keep up with me."

"What about when you settled down with your wife?"

"We never got a chance to settle down," Dan said, and would discuss it no further. Clint decided after that not to even mention the man's wife to him again.

As they traveled farther, Dan Chow suddenly started to ask questions about Clint Adams.

"Why all the interest in me all of a sudden?" Clint asked.

"I do not know how long we will be traveling together," Dan said. "I was simply making an effort to know you a little better."

"I think maybe we found out all we need to know about one another back in that livery stable," Clint said.

"I suspect you are correct."

After that the conversation fell into a lull, and neither man seemed to mind. They had a chance to be alone with their own thoughts, to sort out the consequences of what they were doing—and what they would do.

The first town in Nevada they came to was called Willow Bend. It was little more than a bend in the road, with a small hotel/restaurant and a general store that doubled as a saloon where they went to get a drink before continuing.

One of the things Clint had done during the trip was have Dan Chow describe Rufus King to him, and when the bartenders brought them their beers, Clint asked if a man fitting that description had been through town in the past week or so.

"Let me think," the man said. "We get lots of people through here, and mostly they just have a drink or buy something and move on. I run both the store and the bar, you know, so I see a lot of people. . . ."

And talk all their ears off too, no doubt, Clint thought.

"Could we get back to the description of my friend?" Clint asked.

"Oh, sure," the man said. He was a chunky individual with wire-frame glasses and thinning, brown hair. "This is a friend of yours you're looking for?"

"Yes."

The man looked at Dan Chow and saw that the Oriental had barely touched his beer after an initial sip.

"Something wrong with the beer, friend?" he asked. "Not cold enough for you?"

"I am sure it is fine, for one who likes beer," Dan answered.

"Is there something else I can get you instead?"

"Perhaps some water."

"Sure," the man said, "cold water coming up." He returned with the water and said, "I guess you people don't like anything with liquor in it, huh? I mean, no offense—"

"Could we get back to the original question, please?" Clint asked, cutting the man short for what he hoped would be the last time. "We'd like to get a move on."

"Oh, sure," the man said. "Uh, let me think a minute. Yeah, I think there was a man fitting that description around here last week."

"Did he stay?"

"I don't think so," the man replied. "Not much here to keep a man around, you know."

"Yes, I know," Clint said. He finished his beer and set the empty mug down. "You finished?" he asked Dan.

"Yes," Dan said, pushing the glass of water away. He had taken one sip of that, also.

As they headed for the door the man called out, "There could be something you fellas might be interested in, though."

They stopped and Clint turned and asked, "What's that?"

"There was another man in here looking for your friend," the talkative merchant said.

"When?"

"A couple of hours ago."

Clint and Dan Chow both turned and walked back to the small bar.

"What did he look like?"

"Oh, he was a big one, he was," the man said. "Taller than you, a lot broader, and he was black."

"A black man?" Clint asked.

"Yup, and he was all dressed in black, too," the man added. "Wore a gun on his hip and looked like he knew how to use it."

"What did you tell him?" Clint asked.

"Why, I told him the same thing I told you," the man replied.

"Then if you knew who we were talking about, why did you hesitate, as if you didn't know?"

The man shrugged and looked sheepish. "You've probably guessed that I like to talk. I talk the ears off of most strangers that come through here. That big black fella, though, he didn't want to hear it. All he wanted was his information, so I gave it to him."

So there was somebody else on Rufus King's trail, but was this big black man friend or foe?

"How long ago did this black man leave?"

"He didn't," the man replied.

"He never left?"

"He ain't left yet. He said he was hungry, and was gonna eat before he kept going. I suspect you'll find him over at the hotel."

Clint and Dan exchanged glances, and Clint said, "Could you eat a little something?"

"I could be hungry, yes," Dan answered, and they both turned and left.

"I hope that Chinaman is hungrier than he was thirsty," the man said to the walls.

TWELVE

When they got to the hotel restaurant Clint was mildly surprised to find about a dozen tables, most of which were taken. There was one elderly waiter working the room and he showed Clint and Dan to a table. Across the room they saw the man they were looking for.

"He certainly appears formidable enough," Dan Chow observed.

Even seated the sheer size of the man was apparent. He was at least six four, with wide shoulders and narrow hips. His hands were large, but they appeared to be anything but clumsy. The way the man was sitting, Clint could see the gun on his hip. It was an 1873 Colt Peacemaker, a gun that had formerly been used strictly by the military but had recently become available to the civilian public. It appeared to be a .45 caliber with a seven and a half inch barrel. The gun and the holster it was resting in both appeared to be well cared for.

"If he knows how to use that gun, he's even more formidable," Clint said.

"What can I get you gents?" the old waiter asked.

Clint and Dan both quickly ordered ham and eggs.

"Shall we approach him?" Dan asked.

"Not now," Clint said, "not while he's eating, and besides, I could use something to eat, too. If he starts to leave, we'll approach him.''

When their food came Clint began eating, but Dan virtually ignored his food and kept his eyes on the black man. When the big man finished his meal he sat back and lit a long, slim cigar. At that point, three men entered the room and took the table next to him, and that's when the trouble started.

First, the three men seemed to be heatedly discussing something among themselves. Then gradually, their voices began to rise and become audible to everyone in the room.

"I don't care," one of them was saying. "I don't have to sit in the same room with no nigger while I'm eating."

Clint watched the black very closely, but he seemed to be the only person in the room who didn't hear the remark.

"Didn't you hear me, boy?" the man asked.

No reaction, except to puff contentedly on his cigar.

"Our friend seems to have patience," Clint said.

"It is gradually coming to an end, however," Dan Chow said.

"Hey, nigger, I'm talking to you!" the other man shouted.

When he was still ignored, the man stood up and crossed to the black man's table. His friends rose behind him and moved to back him up, although they seemed to be doing so reluctantly. Clint figured that their friend's big mouth must have gotten them into trouble before.

"I'm talking to you, boy," the man said now, standing directly in front of the black man who finally seemed ready to notice him.

"Yøu talkin' to me?"

"You the only nigger in the room, ain't you?" the man demanded. "And you're smelling it up. I don't like to smell no nigger when I'm eating."

"I'd advise you to eat outside then, friend," the black man said, "because I'm not leavin' until I finish my cigar."

"Is that a fact?" He reached out and plucked the cigar

from the black man's mouth, dropped it to the floor and crushed it with his foot. "Now you can leave."

"Mister, I think you just made the worst mistake of your life." With that the black man stood up swiftly and swung his right arm, landing a backhanded blow on the other man's cheek. The man cried out and went sprawling to the floor, watched in surprise by his two friends.

The man on the floor looked up at the two from his back, his cheek split and bleeding profusely, and said, "Get him!"

They rushed forward towards the black man, who seemed unconcerned.

Clint and Dan Chow watched in fascination as the black man gripped the edge of his table and drove it forward, causing the other side to catch both men at the hips. His strength was such that both men were driven backwards and the wooden tabletop buckled from the force.

The black man pushed aside the broken table and advanced on the two off-balanced men. He grabbed one by the front of his shirt with his right hand and drove his left fist into his stomach. He turned his body sideways then and kicked out at the other man, catching him in the stomach with his right boot heel. Both men folded up and dropped to the floor as if all of the air had been let out of them.

The man on the floor, seeing this, rolled to his left so he could reach the gun on his right hip, and as he did the Gunsmith stood up.

"Don't—" he called out. At the sound of his voice the black man went for his gun, pulling it in an incredibly swift, smooth motion, pivoted and shot the man on the floor before he could reach his gun. He then turned to cover the other two men on the floor, but neither of them had any inclination to go for their guns at the moment.

The black man holstered his gun and stood up straight, then backed up to where his hat was resting on a chair. He picked it up, put it on and motioned for the waiter, who approached hesitantly.

"What do I owe?" he asked.

The waiter handed him a check and he paid it. Then he crossed the room to where Clint was still standing.

"Thanks for the yell," the man said. "I appreciate it."

"No problem," Clint said, "but actually my friend and I were planning on talking to you anyway."

"Oh yeah?" the man said, looking down at Dan Chow. "What about?"

"We understand that you were asking about a man who we are also looking for," Dan said, standing up.

"And who might that be?"

"Rufus King."

"You fellas are looking for Rufus King, too?" the man asked.

"That's right."

"Are you friends of his?"

"No," Dan answered before Clint could stop him. They had no way of knowing whether or not the black man was a friend of King's, and he had hoped to find that out before giving his own reasons for looking for him.

"Well, I'm not either," the man said, "but that don't mean I'm going to tell you guys anything until I know who you are."

Clint looked past the big man at the other three and said, "I have a suggestion."

"What?"

"I don't know if this town has any law or not, but it might be better if we left and found someplace else to talk."

"I can't argue with that," the man said, "but your friend doesn't look like he's finished eating."

"I have completed my meal," Dan Chow said, standing up. "I think it would be wise for us to leave."

"I don't know what you fellas have on your minds, but let's go. My name's Fred Hammer, by the way, but most folks just call me Hammer."

"I am Dan Chow," Dan said.

"And I'm Clint Adams."

"Clint Adams, the Gunsmith?" Hammer asked in surprise.

"That's right."

"Well, let's go, fellas," Hammer said. "I think this is gonna be one real interesting conversation."

THIRTEEN

Hammer was riding a big roan, and they all rode out of town and stopped when they came to a likely looking place for a long conversation.

"Anybody for coffee?" Clint asked.

"Well, I didn't have any back at the hotel," Hammer said. "It was the only thing missing from my meal."

Clint looked at Dan Chow, who nodded. "I'll put some on," Clint said.

They built a fire and when Clint had a pot of coffee on Hammer said, "Well, would you like to tell me why the famous Gunsmith and his Oriental sidekick are interested in me?"

"Actually, we're interested in Rufus King," Clint said. "We just happened to hear that you were also interested in him."

"From that talkative shopkeeper?"

"Yes."

When the coffee was ready Clint poured three cups, but somehow he had the feeling Dan wouldn't drink his.

"I tell you, that man like to talked my head off—and he would have if I hadn't told him to shut up."

"All right," Clint said, taking the hint, "I'll explain."

He told Hammer just why he was looking for Rufus King and when Dan nodded to him, he went on and explained the Chinese man's reasons, as well.

"You gonna kill him when you find him?" Hammer asked.

"I don't know," Clint said.

"I do know," Dan added. "I will kill him."

"You're gonna have to get in line, my friend," Hammer said. "I'm gonna peel that gent's hide off strip by strip."

Dan Chow frowned at Fred Hammer, then said to Clint, "I do not think we need him."

"Who says I need you?" Hammer wanted to know, and he and Dan glared at each other belligerently.

"Now hold on a minute," Clint said. "We're not going to start fighting among ourselves, not when we have a common enemy."

"Let me get this straight," Hammer said to Clint. "You want me to partner up with you two?"

"That's right."

"Why? I mean, why would the Gunsmith want to partner up with anyone, let alone a chink and a nigger."

"We're all looking for the same man," Clint said. "It just doesn't make sense for us to work against each other instead of together."

"Who says I want to work against you?" Hammer asked. "I just want to get there first, is all."

"That's counterproductive."

"It's what?"

"It doesn't make sense for us to race to get to King first when we can all get there together."

"If we all get there together," Hammer asked, "who gets to kill him?"

"I would also like to know the answer to that question," Dan Chow said.

Clint was getting frustrated dealing with the two of them.

"All right, look," he said. "Since you're both so blood-thirsty, when we find him I'll let the two of you go at each other, and the winner gets to kill Rufus King."

He was surprised to find that both of them were taking him seriously.

"I accept those terms," Dan Chow said.

"What?" Hammer asked, and then he started laughing. "Hey, little man, you better be careful—"

He had pointed at Dan Chow with his right hand and taken a step towards him, and the next thing the black man knew he was sailing over the Oriental, through the air, and landed with a fairly earthshaking thud.

As annoyed as Clint had been seconds before, the sight of that big black man sailing over Dan Chow's shoulder was too funny not to laugh at. While Clint was laughing Hammer looked up from the ground at Dan Chow with a stunned look on his face.

Climbing back to his feet Hammer said through his teeth, "Oh, I got to see that one again."

He charged the diminutive Oriental again, and this time Dan Chow moved with him, backwards. Hammer found himself off balance, and then found the other man's feet in his chest, and then he was sailing through the air once again, landing with a painful thump on his back.

Hammer lay there for a few seconds, Clint Adams's laughter ringing in his ears, and then he slowly turned and stared at Dan Chow. Chow stood his ground, his face impassive, as Fred Hammer stood up, more than a full foot taller and probably a good hundred pounds heavier.

"You're really something, aren't you?" Hammer asked. "Well, I'm ready for you now—"

Before Hammer could launch another charge Clint stopped laughing and jumped between them. "All right, Hammer, take it easy."

"Get out of my way, Adams," the black man said. "I've

got to teach this little man a lesson.''

"Look, before you hurt him," Clint said, finding the statement more than a little ironic, "let's all stay healthy enough to find Rufus King.''

Hammer and Dan Chow glared at each other, but Hammer seemed to relax a bit and Clint felt he was past the point of rushing Dan again.

"All right, Adams," Hammer said. "If you're so all fired set on us finding Rufus King together, I'll go along—for now!''

Clint turned to Dan Chow and said, "Dan?"

"Yes. I will go along—also for now.''

"Well, then we're okay," Clint said, and then added to himself, *For now!*

FOURTEEN

Two days later they rode into a town called Cold Steel, Nevada.

"Interesting name," Hammer said, looking at the signpost.

"Yeah," Clint said.

Dan Chow did not comment.

Clint had spent the two days riding between them, and getting between them whenever they threatened to go at one another again. It was obvious by this time that Dan Chow and Fred Hammer were not the best of friends, and might never be, and Clint was starting to be sorry he had hooked up with either of them.

"Why don't we just ride on in," Hammer said, "and see if the town is as interesting as the name."

"Fine," Clint said. "Do you two think you can keep away from each other's throats for a while?"

"Hey, no problem," Hammer said, lighting one of his long, thin cigars.

Clint looked at Dan Chow, who simply looked away, and accepted that as a yes.

"Let's go."

Cold Steel was considerably larger than Willow Bend had

been, and it was bound to take them a little longer to find word on Rufus King.

They dismounted in front of the hotel and Clint suggested they split up and ask around.

"Fine with me," Hammer said. "I'm gonna get a drink, anyway, so I'll check the saloons. Might even find me a girl."

"I will check restaurants and the hotels," Dan Chow said.

"Good," Clint said. That would keep them apart while he wasn't there to keep them from tearing each other apart.

"I'll check in with the sheriff, and then I'll check around at barbershops, bathhouses . . ."

"I'll check the whorehouses," the black man offered.

"That's okay," Clint said. "I'll be able to do it faster."

"Are you saying—?"

"I'm just saying let's stick to the original assignments," Clint said quickly, not wanting to get into an argument with Hammer. So far he'd had enough just refereeing Hammer and Dan's arguments.

"Okay?" he asked.

Hammer stared at him, then shrugged and said, "Okay. I'm thirsty, anyway."

"Let's go, then."

They split up, Clint stopping the first citizen he came to and asking directions to the sheriff's office.

Dan Chow needed no directions to hotels, because they had tied their horses up in front of one. From there he'd certainly receive directions to any other.

Fred Hammer had rarely in his lifetime needed directions to find a saloon.

FIFTEEN

"The Gunsmith?"

Clint closed his eyes, then said to Sheriff Zeb Dewey, "Yes, that's what they call me."

He had walked into the sheriff's office and introduced himself by name, and the lawman had immediately come up with the Gunsmith.

"In my town," the sheriff said. "Damn!"

"Sheriff Dewey," Clint said. He knew the man's name because it was on a board tacked up on the front wall of the jailhouse.

"Yeah?" the man said, looking like he was in a daze.

"Could we talk?"

"Oh, yeah, sure," Dewey said. He had jumped up out of his seat at Clint's introduction, and now he sat back down and said, "Take a seat, Mr. Gun—I mean, Mr. Adams."

"Thanks," Clint said. *Just what I needed*, he thought, *a lawman in awe of a reputation*.

"What can I do for you?" the lawman asked.

"I'm looking for a man who may have passed through your town," Clint explained.

"What's his name?"

"King," Clint answered. "Rufus King."

"King," Dewey repeated.

"Yeah. Know him?"

"It's a fairly common name," the sheriff said.

"How common is Rufus?" Clint asked. Something in the man's manner had changed, and Clint wanted to pursue the matter. "Come on now, Sheriff, either you've heard of the man or you haven't."

The sheriff was obviously experiencing mixed emotions. He was in awe of the Gunsmith, but what were his feelings towards the name Rufus King—or the man, for that matter?

"Sheriff?"

"Uh, yes. King," the lawman said. "I'm thinking . . ."

"Yeah, but what are you thinking about?" Clint asked.

"What do you mean?"

"The name I just gave you means something to you, Sheriff," Clint said. "I'm just trying to find out what."

"I don't know what you mean," Dewey said, standing up. "I know a lot of men named King."

"I'm only interested in one," Clint said, also standing up. "I don't know what your problem is, Sheriff, and I don't really give a damn. Tell me something that'll do me some good, and I'll leave."

Dewey turned around and looked at Clint. "You used to be a lawman."

"Yeah."

"You know it ain't an easy job, right?"

"I know it."

"It's the only thing I know, though," Dewey said.

What am I hearing? Clint asked himself. *Telling me something about Rufus King could cost this man his job?*

"Sheriff—"

"All right," Dewey said. "I'll give you a name, and then I'll tell you something that'll do you some good. The name is

Gallagher, Nate Gallagher. Find him, and finding the Kings will be a lot easier.''

''The Kings?'' Clint said. ''But I want Ru—''

''Now something that'll do you some good,'' Dewey went on.

''What's that?''

''Be careful.''

After Dan Chow left the second hotel, he knew that there was something wrong. As Clint Adams might have said, something funny was going on. Dan Chow preferred to think that it was something peculiar.

Dan was starting to believe that there were people in this town who knew Rufus King and didn't want to say. Both desk clerks that he had spoken to had gotten more than a little nervous at the mention of King's name.

Who was this Rufus King?

He decided to check a couple of restaurants to see if he got the same reactions. Perhaps he should admit to himself that people just didn't like talking to a ''Chinaman,'' but he had the feeling there was more to it than that.

Dan Chow knew that he had the ability to force someone to tell him what he wanted to know, but he preferred not to do that.

Not until he had to.

''Well, I always wondered if what they said about you people was true,'' the blond girl said to Hammer.

''Oh, yeah? What's that?''

''Well, you know,'' the girl said, staring up at him from between his legs. ''That you had big ones.''

''Well, they were wrong, I guess,'' Hammer said.

''What do you mean, wrong?'' she asked, wrapping both

of her hands around his erect penis.

"I don't have big ones," he said. "I've just got *a* big one."

"I'll say," she said.

With that she leaned over and took the huge, bulbous head of his penis into her mouth. It felt good, but it wasn't what he wanted.

"Look," he said, grabbing her beneath the arms, "save this for someone else. There's only one thing I want right now."

"And what's that?" she asked, coyly.

"I want to know where to find Rufus King," he said.

The girl's head snapped up as if someone had slapped her across the face. "What?"

"I heard that he spends time with you when he's in town," Hammer said.

"Who told you that?" she demanded.

"Somebody," he said. Actually, it was one of the other girls down in the saloon who had given him the information, under the condition that he not give her name out. The second condition was that he visit her in her room before he left town, a condition he gladly agreed to. This girl with him now was not his type. She was blonde, but she was a little too plump for him, and the other girl was a redhead with a lean, finely toned body.

But that was for later.

"Well, somebody lied," the girl said, sitting up in bed.

"I don't think so."

"Look, mister, if you don't wanna fuck, then I gotta go back downstairs." She got off the bed and started to put her dress back on.

"Little girl," he said, "I'd hate to have to make you tell me what I want to know."

The menace in his voice made her look at him again.

"Look, mister, there ain't no cause to threaten me. I get enough of that from—"

"From whom?" he asked. "King? You afraid of him?"

"Look, mister," she said, putting on her shoes, "I can send one of the other girls up here to take care of you, because all you seem to want to do to me is talk."

"That ain't all I'm going to do to you, woman, you can count on that."

She was afraid of Rufus King, so all Hammer figured he had to do was make her fear him even more.

"I'll spend some time up here with one of the other girls for a while, which will give you time to think about who you should be more afraid of, Rufus King, who isn't here, or me, who is."

She stared at him wide-eyed, a big black man with a mean face and big hands—and a huge, throbbing erection—and then she backed towards the door, groping behind her for the doorknob.

"When I'm finished with one of your girlfriends," he added, "I'll come downstairs for you, girlie. Count on it!"

SIXTEEN

The blonde wasn't gone two minutes before the door opened and the redhead stepped in. When she saw Hammer lying on the bed with a full grown erection the likes of which she had never seen before, her eyes widened and her jaw dropped.

"Isn't your girlfriend going to be a little suspicious," he asked, "you sneaking up here right after she left?"

"She ain't my friend," the redhead said, approaching the bed, "and she won't be suspicious. I just happened to be standing at the foot of the steps when she came running down saying you wanted another girl." She reached behind her to undo her dress, then dropped it to the floor and said, "Here I am."

While she divested herself of the rest of her clothes, he watched in admiration. She had high, firm, brown-tipped breasts, a flat tummy and long, elegant legs.

She sat on the bed next to him and asked, "What did you do to her, anyway? She looked like she'd seen the devil."

"I just asked her a question."

"About Rufus King?"

"That's right."

"Honey, nobody in this town will talk about the Kings," she said.

"What do you mean, *the Kings?* There's more than one?"

"There sure is. That's a big family, and everybody in Nevada knows them."

"You know them?"

"I know about them," she said. "A meaner bunch of people you'd never want to meet."

"Then you know where they live?" he asked, taking one of her fine breasts in his hand like it was a piece of fruit.

"Ha, nobody knows that."

"You just said they're well known," Hammer said. "You mean they don't have a big ranch somewhere?"

"Hell, they're not ranchers," the girl said, "they're bad men. You know, desperados."

"I get the picture."

"Nobody finds them unless they wanna be found," she said, reaching out to run her fingers lightly over the head of his penis.

"You mean there's nobody in this town who might know where Rufus King is heading?"

"Well, maybe one person," she said.

"The girl. What's her name?"

"Amy? No, she don't know. King would never tell one of his girls. Nah, I was talking about Nate Gallagher."

"Who's that?"

"A guy who used to ride with Rufus when they were younger. Now he's just kind of a message carrier, you know?"

"Then all I've got to do is find this guy Gallagher."

"I should warn you," she said, "if you find Rufus, you're bound to find the rest of his family, too. I'd be careful if I was you."

"Honey, I was born careful," he said, squeezing her

breast. She closed her eyes and moaned, closing her fist around his cock.

"What's your name?" he asked.

"Carla."

"Well, Carla honey, why don't you get yourself on up here and see if you can't do something about this condition of mine."

"That would be my pleasure, big fella," she said, climbing aboard him, one knee on each side, so that she pinned his erection to his belly with her crotch. She moved her hips back and forth so that her pubic hair and lips were rubbing up and down the long length of his cock.

"I hope you don't mind if I hurry this along a little," he said, grabbing her by the hips, "but I've waited long enough as it is."

"Be my—ohhh, God!" she cried as he lifted her up and impaled her on him. "God, I've never felt anything so huge . . ."

"It's all yours, darlin'," he said, "every hungry inch of it."

He closed his eyes, surrendering himself to the sensation of her hot, wet flesh closing around him, pulling on him as she rode him up and down.

"Oh, Jesus, this is—I can't believe this—" she was babbling as her bouncing became more and more frenzied. "I'm going to go out of my mind . . ."

"Easy, lady, easy," he said, reaching for her. He pulled her down so he could press his mouth to hers, and feel her hardened nipples scraping his chest.

He closed his hands around the cheeks of her ass and began to grind her into him, and as they both built to a shattering climax, the door to the room was kicked open and men seemed to flood into the room.

"Wha—" Hammer said, pushing the girl off of him and onto the floor.

His gunbelt was hanging on the bedpost and as he reached for it one of the men shouted, "You'll never make it, nigger!"

Hammer felt the same way. He never would make it, but he had to give it a try.

When the window shattered inward, everyone looked towards it but Hammer. He had trained himself over the years to take advantage of the most unexpected situations.

Clint Adams entered the room in a shower of glass, gun blazing as fast as he could trigger it. Hammer grabbed his Peacemaker and threw himself off the bed to his left, firing as quickly as he could thumb the hammer.

The group of surprised men began to stagger back as lead struck them, and some of them spilled out into the hallway where they were met by the flying feet and *shuriken* of Dan Chow.

Then it was quiet, except for the pitiful sound being made by the wounded men who were littering the floor. There were some others who could make no sounds, because they were dead.

Hammer stood up, unmindful of his nakedness, and stared at Clint Adams. Dan Chow came through the door and stared at Hammer.

"We saw them go into the saloon," Clint asked, "and we figured it just had to be you."

"I'm glad you figured," Hammer said.

"What was their beef?"

"I'm not sure," Hammer said. He walked to where his clothes were by the bed and fished out one of his long cigars. After he had it lit he looked down at the frightened, naked redhead and said, "What do you know about this, Carla?"

"Me?" she asked. "I don't know anything, I swear."

"She had me pretty much occupied when they broke in," Hammer said.

"I don't wonder," Clint said, admiring Carla's charms.

"I swear, mister—" she said.

"Take it easy, Carla," Hammer said. "I've got enough faith in my own ability to attract women that I half believe you."

"We might as well wait here for the law to show up," Clint said. "You've got time to get dressed, Hammer."

"Huh?" Hammer asked, taking his cigar out of his mouth. Then he looked down at himself and said, "Oh, yeah."

As he dressed he said, "I'm obliged to the both of you, although I didn't hear our Oriental friend fire a shot."

"He doesn't have to," Clint said.

"I believe that," Hammer said, having had firsthand experience of Dan Chow's talents. "What did you fellas find out?"

"A name," Clint said. "Nate Gallagher. My source says he might be able to point us towards Rufus King."

"Hey, I got the same name," Hammer said, pulling his boots on. "Was your source willing?"

"Oh, yeah," Clint said, "as long as I don't reveal it."

"Yeah," Hammer said, looking at the girl, "mine was pretty willing, too."

"I, too, received the name Gallagher," Dan Chow said. "Alas, my source was not so willing."

After Dan had checked the restaurants with no success, he had felt compelled to go back to one of the desk clerks—it didn't much matter which—and ask his questions again, under different circumstances.

"Well, it looks like we all struck pay dirt," Hammer said. "Now all we got to do is get out of this town with a man named Gallagher."

"That may not be easy," Clint said. "If these men were friends of King's, there may be more."

"Well, there's more than one King, I can tell you that," Hammer said, strapping on his gun. "According to my source, there's an army of them, just about."

"Yeah, the sher— uh, my source did say something about Kings," Clint said.

"Jesus Christ!" Clint's source said, walking through the door. "What the hell happened up here?"

"Just a little misunderstanding, Sheriff," Clint said. "I'm just not sure what it was about."

Dewey turned to his deputy, who had come in behind him and said, "See how many of these idiots are still alive, and then get some men to take them to the doctor's office."

"Right, Sheriff."

"It was self-defense, Sheriff," Hammer said. "The girl can testify to that."

Dewey looked down at Carla who said, "That's right, Sheriff. Self-defense."

Dewey stared at her for a long moment, then said, "Get your clothes on, girl."

They all watched as she did so, and then Dewey told her to leave.

"Bye, Carla," Hammer said. "I'll stop by next time I'm through this way."

Carla stared at him, part of her wanting him to stay away and part of her—the wet part between her legs—wanting him to come back.

"Get out, girl," the sheriff said wearily.

Clint ejected the spent cartridges from his gun and replaced them with live ones before holstering his gun, and Hammer did the same.

"Some of those men in the hall have got some kind of funny looking metal star between their eyes," Dewey said, looking puzzled.

"Those are mine," Dan Chow said. "I will retrieve them."

He backed into the hall and then reappeared, tucking his *shuriken* behind the wide belt around his waist.

"Adams," Sheriff Dewey said, "you and your friends

better mount up and ride out of town right now, before I change my mind. Consider this professional courtesy towards an ex-lawman.''

''I appreciate that, Sheriff,'' Clint said, ''but we really can't leave until we see a man called Nate Gallagher.''

''That's easy,'' Dewey said.

''Good,'' Hammer said, happily.

''You'll take us to him?'' Clint asked, puzzled as to why Dewey was being so helpful now when he wasn't before.

''I don't have to take you to him, Mr. Adams,'' Sheriff Dewey said. ''He's right at your feet.''

Clint looked down at the man who was lying at his feet, the first one he'd shot when he'd come through the window. Sightless eyes stared up at him accusingly.

''That's Gallagher?'' he said.

''That was Nate Gallagher,'' the lawman said.

SEVENTEEN

"All right," Clint said, "let's see what we've got to work with."

They were sitting around their fire, waiting for their dinner of beans and coffee to be ready. They had left town immediately upon finding out that Nate Gallagher was dead, traveled until darkness fell and then made camp.

"What we got is nothing," Hammer said in disgust.

"Don't be such a pessimist," Clint said.

"Religion ain't got nothing to do with it," the black man said.

Clint stared at him, trying to decide whether he was serious or not. "Look, we learned a few things about Rufus King that might help us find him."

"Sure," Hammer said. "He likes plump blondes."

"He has family," Clint said.

"That's encouraging," Hammer said. "All that means is that he's likely not to be alone when we find him."

"It does not matter," Dan Chow said. "I will still kill him, no matter how much family he has."

"There he goes again," Hammer told Clint. "Why does he keep insisting that he's gonna kill King?"

"Forget it," Clint said. "He's just showing a positive attitude."

"Well, I can be pretty positive, too," Hammer said. "Like I'm positive this Chinaman is gonna have to go through me to get to King."

"There *you* go again," Clint said, "setting us against each other."

"It's his fault, damn it!" Hammer said.

"He hardly says a word," Clint argued.

"And when he does he says, 'I'm gonna kill Rufus King,' " Hammer said, pitching his deep voice higher.

"You know, you two are going to end up killing each other," Clint said. "Maybe I should let you go ahead and do that."

"And then what?" Hammer asked. "You'll kill King?"

"I told you I haven't decided what I'm going to do yet," Clint said.

"Yeah, yeah, so you say."

"I'm not going to argue with you, Hammer," Clint said. He stood up and said, "Let's split the watch."

"I will not sleep," Dan Chow said.

"You know," Hammer said, "everytime he opens his mouth he gets my goat. What's the matter, Chinaman. You don't need sleep like the rest of us mortals?"

Dan looked at Hammer and shrugged. "I am not sleepy."

"Shit," Hammer said. "I am."

Later that night, Hammer opened his eyes and sat up. Try as he did, he couldn't get to sleep.

"Shit," he said again.

Clint was awake, too, but he remained lying down, watching Hammer as he approached Dan Chow.

"Any coffee left?" Hammer asked, crouching down by the fire.

"I assume so," Dan said. "I have not had any."

"No, I don't suppose you have," Hammer said, pouring himself a cup.

Dan Chow continued to stare out into the darkness while Hammer drank his coffee, studying the little Oriental.

"Those things you throw," Hammer said, breaking the silence.

"They are called *shuriken*," Dan Chow said without looking at the black man.

"Yeah, well, whatever," Hammer replied. "What are they, round knives, or something?"

"Would you like to see one?"

"Hell, yes. I'm always interested in a different kind of weapon."

Dan slipped one out from behind his belt and handed it to Hammer. "Do not cut your finger."

"Hell, Chinaman," Hammer said, "I've been handling knives since I was—ouch, god damn it!"

He took a quick look at Dan Chow to see if he was laughing, but the Chinese was still looking out into the darkness. Hammer licked the blood from his punctured finger, then held the *shuriken* by its shiny center and inspected its five razor-sharp points.

"How do you throw these things so accurately?" he asked.

"You flick them, backhand," Dan said.

"Backhanded?" Hammer asked. He held the star and tried it in slow motion. "I'd cut my hand open trying to do that."

"Yes," Dan Chow said, "you would."

"Uh, listen . . . Dan."

"Yes?"

"Would you—uh, could you teach me how to throw these things?" Hammer asked.

Dan Chow didn't answer.

"I mean, I'd pay you to teach me."

"I do not want your money," the little Oriental said.

"Well," Hammer said then, "I could teach you something in return. You know, like a trade?"

Dan Chow seemed to be thinking that offer over, and then he asked, "What could you possibly teach me?"

"I could teach you how to shoot," Hammer said.

"I already know how to shoot."

"I could teach you how to, uh, get along with women," Hammer offered.

Dan Chow said, "I have no need of such knowledge."

"Jesus," Hammer said, wracking his brain, and then he said, "I've got it. I could teach you something that no one is better qualified to teach you."

That got Dan Chow's attention, and he turned his head to look at Hammer. "What is that?"

Hammer grinned and said, "I could teach you to be black!"

Dan Chow studied Hammer impassively for several seconds, then looked off into the darkness and said, "You have a deal."

EIGHTEEN

The next morning while Clint made breakfast, Dan Chow took Hammer aside and began giving him lessons in throwing the *shuriken*. Clint listened while Dan explained that the *shuriken* was actually a Japanese weapon, and not Chinese, but Hammer was less concerned with its history than he was with learning to throw it accurately.

When Clint called them over for breakfast, Hammer approached winding a bandana around his right hand.

"Catch a few nicks?" he asked the big black man.

"I hope I can learn to throw those things before I lose my fingers," Hammer said.

"I hope you can still use the hand."

"I can hold a fork," Hammer assured him.

"I was more worried about you holding a gun," Clint said. "We might need it."

"Don't worry about that," Hammer said. "Worse comes to worse, I can shoot left-handed."

"Is that a fact?" Clint said, handing him a plate with bacon and biscuits. "You're a man of many talents, Hammer."

"You got that right."

"And not exactly modest about it, either."

"I leave that for other people," Hammer replied, grinning.

Clint handed Dan Chow a plate, and the Oriental took it and began eating in silence.

"Maybe I shouldn't be asking this, Hammer," Clint said, sitting down with a plate of his own, "but why are you after Rufus King?"

All traces of humor faded from Hammer's face, and his eyes turned cold. "You're right, Adams. You shouldn't be asking."

"We've told you why we're looking for him," Clint reasoned.

"That was your choice," Hammer answered. "I didn't force either one of you to do that. My choice is to keep my business to myself. Just be sure of one thing. When I find him, I'm gonna peel his hide off."

"That's the second time you've said that," Clint said. "Don't you mean that you're going to kill him?"

"I mean what I say," Hammer said. "He may die while I'm peeling him, but I'm gonna peel him."

With that Hammer fell as silent as Dan Chow and both men ate their meals in stony-faced silence.

Clint missed Duke at that moment. At least if the big fella was there he'd have someone to talk to.

After breakfast they broke camp and saddled their horses.

"What's the next town?" Hammer asked.

"I haven't been in Nevada in some time," Clint replied, "but I think it's a town called Cord."

Shaking his head Hammer said, "Where the hell do they get these names from?"

As they started their horses towards Cord, Clint said, "Listen, Hammer, if we're going to be riding together, I don't want any hard feelings. I'm sorry if I was prying into your personal business—''

Hammer held up his wrapped hand to stop Clint and said, ''Forget it. Maybe later I'll tell you fellas about it, but not right now. Okay?''

''Sure,'' Clint said.

Clint looked over at Dan Chow and saw that he had strapped on an old Navy Colt. The Oriental saw that he was being watched and said, ''Perhaps you were right.''

''About what?'' Hammer asked.

''I suggested he wear the gun, in case we run into some long-range trouble that his star knives can't handle.''

''He does pretty good with those things,'' Hammer said, sounding as if he were coming to Dan Chow's defense, which was a switch.

''Well,'' Clint said, ''if he can use the gun half as well as he throws those things, we'll be all right.''

Hammer looked expectantly at Dan Chow. ''I can hit what I aim at,'' he assured them.

''See?'' Hammer said to Clint. ''He's okay.''

''Yeah,'' Clint said. Maybe he wouldn't have to come between these two as much as he'd had to up until now. They seemed to have formed some sort of a friendship.

''Let's get going, then,'' Clint said. ''We don't want King getting too far ahead of us. If he's got family, or a gang, here in Nevada, we want to reach him before he gets to them.''

''That would seem to make sense,'' Dan Chow said.

''Well, as long as we're all agreed,'' Hammer said, ''let's move out.''

All agreed, Clint thought. That was almost too good to be true.

They rode single file, with Clint taking the point, and he

took the opportunity the solitude offered to do some thinking about Rufus King.

The man seemed to have more friends in Nevada than enemies. In fact, Clint, Hammer and Dan Chow seemed to be the only enemies he had in the state. Yet, King and his family had been described as "bad men." What he had done to Clint, and Dan Chow's wife—and the Gunsmith didn't know that full story any more than he knew Hammer's—seemed to qualify King for that description. It seemed likely that the people they'd run across so far weren't so much King's allies as they were afraid of him.

Rufus King was about to leave the town of Cord, Nevada when he got a telegram from Cold Steel. It was delivered to a room above the saloon, where King had spent the night with a girl named Rosalie. She wasn't a blonde—King didn't have a blonde in Cord—but she was on the plump side, with big breasts and heavy thighs and buttocks.

As he turned her over in bed to plow her from behind, there was a knock on the door.

"Who is it?" he called out.

"Telegram, Rufe," a man called out.

King got off the bed and opened the door of the room, giving the man in the hall an unobstructed view of the naked girl.

"Come on, come on," King said, prodding the man with his right hand.

"Oh," Davey Cannon said, tearing his eyes from the girl's wide ass. "I thought you'd like to see this before you left town, Rufe."

Davey Cannon had been trying to join the King gang since he had turned eighteen, a year before. Whenever Rufus King was in Cord, Cannon did his best to try to impress the older man.

King, a tall, gangly man of thirty, accepted the telegram and read it. He was as unmindful of his own nakedness as he was of the girl's, whose ass was still in the air, awaiting Rufus King's attention. Cannon took the opportunity to inspect the girl while King read the telegram.

It was from the blond girl in Cold Steel, informing King that a big black man, a small Chinaman and a tall white man were on his trail. They had killed Nate Gallagher and five other men, and were on their way to Cord.

King looked at Cannon, who was ogling the girl, and tapped him lightly on the side of the face.

"Huh?"

"Get some men, Cannon," he said. "A lot of men."

"Sure," Davey Cannon said. "What am I getting them for?"

"For trouble," King said.

"Making some or avoiding some?"

"We're gonna cause some for three fellas who are looking for some," King said. "We're gonna give them all they can handle, so you get me some good men, huh?"

"The best, Rufe," Davey said. "The best."

"Then get going."

With a last, mournful look at the girl's upturned buttocks, Davey Cannon took off down the hall to do as he was told. This, he was sure, would be enough to get him into the King family.

King closed the door and turned his attention back to the girl on the bed.

"Honey, my behind is getting tired," she complained.

"Don't worry, sweetheart," he said, "I'll get to it."

A black man, a Chinaman and a white man, he thought, getting on the bed behind the girl. Placing one hand on each of her hips, he tried to remember if he knew anyone that fit those descriptions. A white man, that could be anyone. A

Chinaman? There was the Chinese girl he'd had a few months back, could be a boyfriend of hers on his trail. The black? He hadn't killed any black men lately, so it might have just been a bounty hunter.

Thrusting himself into the girl, who moaned aloud in appreciation, he decided it didn't really matter much. With the reception he was going to set up for them before leaving town, they'd be dead before he reached the next one.

NINETEEN

When Clint, Hammer and Dan Chow reached Cord's main street, the Gunsmith's sixth sense was working overtime.

"Hold it," Clint said.

"What is it?" Dan Chow asked.

"Something's up," Clint said.

"Yeah," Hammer said. "The street's too empty."

"A trap?" Dan asked.

"Looks like," Clint said.

"Somebody from Cold Steel sent the word on ahead," Hammer said. "He knows we're after him now, and he's waiting for us."

"Not necessarily," Clint said.

"What do you mean?"

"Somebody's waiting for us," Clint said, "but King could have left town long ago."

"In that case, there's no sense in us riding into this little trap," Hammer said.

"All we need is one person who can give us some information," Clint said.

"How do we do that?" Hammer asked.

"Preferably without riding into this," Clint said, indicating the empty street ahead of them.

"How?" Dan Chow asked.

"Well, if nobody else has an idea . . ." Clint said, and went on to explain what he had in mind.

TWENTY

Davey Cannon had a man on almost every building on Main Street. He himself was on the roof of the hotel, the highest structure in town, but he was feeling even higher than that. Rufus King's last words to him had Davey's head in the clouds.

"Do this right, Cannon, and you're in," King had said to him, and Davey was repeating those words to himself over and over again, when he should have been keeping alert.

Clint, Hammer and Dan Chow tied their horses outside of town, and each man entered town on foot from a different direction. The plan was simple. Each man was to locate one man each who was part of the trap, question him quietly as to who had organized it, and find out where that man was, whether it was Rufus King or someone else. If King was gone, then hopefully the man left in charge would be able to tell them where to find him.

Hammer saw a man on the roof of the general store. Using the rear steps, he climbed onto the roof from behind and was on the man before he had a chance to react.

With Hammer's rock hard arm beneath his neck, the man had no choice but to talk or have his neck broken.

Dan Chow found a man on the roof of the single-story town bank. Using his own special abilities, he scaled the back wall and was on his man before he knew what hit him. A short blow to the kidney robbed the man of any opportunity to make a sound, and then Dan took hold of the man's throat and gently but firmly squeezed the information out of him.

Clint found his man on the roof of the livery, and made his way up there through the inside. The man heard him coming, but when he turned around he found himself looking down the barrel of the Gunsmith's modified .45, and wanted to live too much to cry out.

He also wanted to live too much to keep quiet when he was asked a question.

Clint left him unconscious and met Hammer and Dan Chow behind the hotel.

"I guess we all got the information," Clint said.

"All my man knew was that a Davey Cannon put him up on the roof and described us to him. There was money in it for him if we rode in, and didn't ride out."

"My man wanted the money," Dan Chow said, "but he was also too afraid of the Kings not to go along."

"Well," Clint said, "let's get up on this roof and talk to the man in charge."

"There's a side door," Hammer said.

"Let's try it."

The side door led to a stairway, and using that they got to the second floor, and then the roof without running into anybody.

"The whole *town* can't be in on it," Hammer said.

"They could," Clint said, "but maybe they just knew trouble was brewing and decided to stay out of it."

They found a hatch in the hall leading to the roof, and it was open.

"We've got to keep him from sounding the alarm," Clint said, "so we'll have to hit him fast."

"I will go up first," Dan Chow said.

"Why you?" Hammer asked. "I took care of my man without him hearing me."

"I am smaller," Dan Chow said. "You can lift me up through the hatch."

"I can jump up there and grab both sides and haul myself up," Hammer said.

"You fellas want to flip a coin?" Clint asked. "Hammer, let's lift Dan up and let him handle it. Okay?"

"Sure," Hammer said. "Let's just get it done."

Together he and Clint lifted Dan Chow up and through the hatch, and then they followed. By the time Hammer climbed through and pulled Clint up, Dan had Davey Cannon down on the roof, holding one of his arms up behind him, and pressing his foot into the side of his neck.

Hammer and Clint approached and looked down at Cannon.

"He's just a kid," Hammer said.

"And a scared kid at that," Clint said. He crouched down and put his face where the kid could see it. "Listen, son. My friend here is going to take his foot off your neck and let you up, and then we're going to have a talk. Okay?"

The kid nodded as best he could with Dan Chow's foot holding him down.

"If you try and yell, one of my two friends will break your neck, and I won't be able to stop them. Understood?"

The kid made a gurgling sound and attempted another nod.

"Okay, Dan," Clint said, straightening up, "let him up and let's see what he's got to tell us."

What Davey Cannon had to tell the trio they already knew, so he wasn't much of a help.

"You wasn't supposed to leave town alive," he said, and Dan Chow put him to sleep.

"Big deal," Hammer said as they made their way back through the hotel to the ground floor. "This is starting to get more than a little frustrating."

"And what's worse is that King knows we're on his trail," Clint said.

"That will make it more difficult," Dan Chow agreed.

"We can discuss how much more difficult later," Clint said. "Let's get moving before the kid or one of the others comes to and sounds the alarm."

TWENTY-ONE

The three men bypassed the town of Cord, giving it a wide berth, leaving behind a group of puzzled men wondering what they were doing sitting on rooftops armed to the teeth. When Davey Cannon finally woke up, he was a very unhappy young man, and actually hoped that he would never meet Rufus King again—for reasons of his health.

They rode on until darkness began to fall, then camped and discussed their situation.

"It's been discouraging," Clint admitted, "but I'm not ready to give up."

"That statement indicates that eventually you will be ready to quit," Dan Chow said. "I will never give up."

"Neither will I," Hammer said. "All King is doing is getting me madder."

"All right, then," Clint said, "let's discuss the newest developments. King knows we're coming."

"He knows that *someone* is coming," Dan Chow amended.

"Hell, man," Hammer said, "how hard is it to figure? He

95

knows there's a black man, a yellow man and a white man. He's got to know you," Hammer added, directing the remark to Dan Chow.

"I was thinking the same thing about you," Dan said.

"Uh-uh," Hammer said, shaking his head. "We've never had the pleasure of meeting. If we had, he'd be dead and we wouldn't be going through this."

"Dan?" Clint said.

Dan Chow shook his head and said, "Would that we had met, but we have not."

"Well, I've never seen King," Clint said, "and for all we know he still thinks I'm dead."

"Then all he knows is that three different color men are trailing him," Hammer said.

"And we stand out like a fox in a chicken coop," Clint said. "Spotting us won't exactly be hard, which means it'll be easy for him to keep setting traps for us."

The three of them fell silent and exchanged glances for a few moments before Clint put into words what was on all of their minds. "Maybe we ought to split up."

They digested that for a while over their dinner and coffee, and then Hammer spoke up. "Splitting up would help you the most, Clint. Dan and I would still be easy to spot."

"I do not know if we should split up," Dan said. "There is strength in numbers, and we know that King will be setting traps for us along the way."

"He's bound to get word from Cord about what happened, so the rest of our trip is going to be no picnic."

"We might have a better chance of making it out of Nevada alive if we stick together," Hammer said.

"That would seem to make sense," Dan Chow said.

"We're all agreed, then," Clint said. "We'll stay together."

Dan Chow nodded, and Hammer said, "Besides, I ain't quite got the hang of throwing them star knives, yet."

"*Shuriken*," Dan Chow said.

"Whatever," Hammer said.

TWENTY-TWO

Tempted to bypass the next town, they decided against it, just on the off chance that King would be there.

"Maybe he'll take charge of his own trap this time," Hammer said.

"If there is one," Clint said.

"What do you mean?"

"I can't believe that King will be able to throw an army at us in every town we come to," Clint said. "There's just not that many men ready to commit murder for his benefit."

"Are you saying that you think we should just ride into the next town?" Hammer asked.

"No, I'm not saying that," Clint said. "I am suggesting, however, that one of us ride in ahead of the other two, and signal if everything looks okay."

"Which of us are you suggesting goes first?" Dan Chow asked.

"I'm kind of interested in that myself," Hammer answered.

"I think we settled that last night," Clint said. "You two are just as distinctive individually as we all are collectively. I'll ride in ahead and come back for you two if the coast is clear."

Hammer and Dan Chow exchanged glances, and the big black man shrugged. "I'll go for it."

"I think perhaps if we are to repeat this process in every town we come to," Dan Chow said, "it would only be fair to alternate who the first man in town will be."

"I'm not as easy to spot as you two," Clint argued.

"Maybe not," Hammer said, "but I agree with Dan. It's not fair to you to have you take that risk every time."

"If that's the way you fellas feel, I won't argue," Clint said.

"We are partners, after all," Dan Chow said. "Or at least, we will be until we find Rufus King."

Clint was reminded of how much both Hammer and Dan Chow wanted to kill Rufus King, and wondered if when they did find their man, the two "partners" would actually go at one another for that honor.

And what of his own intentions upon finding King? Maybe it was time for him to decide. Did he want to kill him? And if that was the case, would he be willing to fight Hammer and Dan Chow for the privilege?

He still didn't know Hammer's reasons for wanting to kill King so badly, but he knew Dan Chow's reason well. Did his own reasons stack up against Dan Chow's? Did the shooting of a man's horse rank with the death of a man's wife?

As much as Duke meant to the Gunsmith, he could not in all conscience answer that question with a yes. So, when they did find Rufus King, Clint Adams wanted to know if King had tried to kill him for himself, or for some other reason. After that, it was up to Hammer and Dan Chow.

TWENTY-THREE

Clint rode into the town of Albano, Nevada with all of his senses alive for any signs of danger. The muscles of his stomach and back were painfully clenched against the possibility of a bullet. His eyes scanned the streets, the alleys, the rooftops, but in one sense he was put at some sort of ease by the fact that there was activity in the streets. There were wagons, horses, men, women and children, and if there was any chance of trouble, these people would have had to know it, and they wouldn't be out in the open like that.

Clint actually rode from one end of the town to the other, and then back again to signal Hammer and Dan Chow that it was all clear and they could come down.

It had also been decided that Clint wouldn't wait for them, but would go his own way once he'd signaled them. Having done so, Clint turned Lance back around and rode to the first saloon he'd seen, called the Albano Saloon.

Tying Lance up outside Clint grabbed his rifle and carried it with him. If there *was* going to be trouble, he wanted as much firepower at his disposal as possible. To that end he also had his .22 caliber New Line Colt tucked into his waistband, inside his shirt.

As he approached the bar the bartender looked at him expectantly.

"Beer," Clint said. The bartender nodded and moved to get it for him.

Keeping his back to the room Clint nevertheless looked it over, using the mirror behind the bar. Nobody seemed to be paying special attention to him, and nobody seemed to be making a special effort *not* to pay attention to him.

"Here ya go," the bartender said, putting a frothy mug of beer down in front of him.

"Thanks," Clint said, dropping a coin on the bar.

Apparently not a member of the fraternity of talkative bartenders, the man moved to the far end of the bar and leaned against it lazily, waiting for his next customer.

The Gunsmith's extra sense, which rarely failed him, was not acting up at the moment, and finally his stomach muscles unclenched.

At that moment the batwing doors swung inward to admit a big black man, who did attract the attention of the room full of men.

Hammer was watched as he approached the bar at the furthest end from the Gunsmith. The bartender watched the black man with wide eyes, and when Hammer spoke it was the kind of remark Clint had come to expect from him.

"I ain't gonna bite you, friend," he said to the bartender. "All I want's a beer."

The bartender stared, and Hammer asked, "You do serve black folks, don't you?"

"Uh, I don't know, rightly," the man finally replied. "Ain't never had none in here before."

"Well, you have now," Hammer told him, "and I'd like a cold beer . . . please."

Clint's grin was as imperceptible as the shaking of his head as he watched the nervous bartender serve the big black man.

"Thank you kindly," Hammer said. He dropped a coin on the bar and the bartender examined it closely. Hammer leaned toward the man and said, "Don't worry, black folks' money is just the same as white folks'."

The bartender nodded jerkily, and moved towards the center of the bar, where he was standing away from Clint and Hammer, and with some townsmen. He immediately fell into conversation with the men, and it was plain that they were talking about Hammer.

Clint looked around, but Dan Chow had not yet entered the saloon. He wondered what degree of interest the Chinese would elicit, in comparison to Hammer.

"Another beer," he called to the barkeep.

"Sure."

When the bartender returned and placed the beer in front of him Clint said, "Don't rush away."

He stopped and stared.

"Not very talkative, are you?"

"No."

"Well, maybe you can talk long enough to tell me if a friend of mine has been through here in the past few days."

"Who would that be?" the man asked.

"Rufus King."

The bartender's eyes narrowed and he said, "You're a friend of Rufus King's?"

"That's right."

"Mister," the bartender said, "I wouldn't go saying something like that too loud in this town."

"Why is that?"

"The Kings ain't welcome in this town, least of all Rufus King."

"Is that a fact?" Clint asked. "Then I guess he hasn't been through this way."

"If he had, he'd be dead," the man said, "and you will be

too if you don't watch your step.''

"Is that a threat?''

"I ain't a man to threaten, mister," the bartender said.
"I'm just giving you some good advice." Suddenly, the
bartender looked past Clint and, eyes wide, cried out, "Not
in here, Jeb!''

Clint turned quickly and drew his gun, firing by instinct.
The man with the gun moved at the last moment, saving his
life. The Gunsmith's bullet smashed into the other man's
gun, sending it spinning to the floor.

Several others stood up and seemed about to draw their
weapons, but Hammer's deep voice called out, "I
wouldn't!''

They looked his way and found that they were covered by
the black man's gun as well.

Suddenly it seemed that almost every man in the saloon
was prepared to draw on Hammer and Clint.

"That would not be an advisable course of action, my
friends," another voice said, and it came from the balcony
above the saloon's main floor. Clint glanced up there and saw
Dan Chow standing with his gun in his hand.

"You, behind the bar," the Oriental said. "Please put
both hands out where I can see them.''

The bartender obeyed, placing both of his hands on the
bar's surface.

"It looks like we got ourselves a whole different problem
here," Hammer said.

"It gets more and more confusing, doesn't it?" Clint
asked.

The first man who drew his gun was standing bent over,
cradling his right hand. The other men in the room were
standing around, exchanging glances, waiting for someone
to take the initiative.

Clint decided he'd best take it away before someone got

brave. He looked at the man who drew, who was barely eighteen if he was a day. "You're lucky you're not a hand with a gun, son, or you'd be dead by now," Clint said to him.

"More like you'd be," the boy said between his teeth. "Coming in here saying the name of Rufus King like that, claiming to be his friend."

"We can explain that," Clint said, "but I think it's time to bring the law into this before the situation gets out of hand and a lot of people get hurt. Don't you agree, bartender?" Clint asked.

"Yes, sir."

"Good. Then you go and fetch the sheriff and tell him we could all use some help over here to avoid bloodshed, because the last thing I want to do is kill someone."

"And the last thing I want to do," Hammer interjected, "is get killed."

As the bartender hurried out to get the sheriff Clint said, "Yeah, there's that, too."

TWENTY-FOUR

When Sheriff Randall Hitchcock entered the Albano Saloon he could feel the tension in the air. The plateau he found himself facing was as potentially explosive as any he'd ever encountered in his thirty years as a lawman.

He spotted the white man and the black man immediately, facing the roomful of men with their guns drawn, and then he looked up and noticed the Chinaman on the balcony.

"What the hell is going on here?" he demanded.

"Ah, Sheriff," Clint said, "I'm glad you got here so quickly."

"Can I get an explanation as a reward?" the sheriff demanded.

"That young man," Clint said, indicating the kid who was holding his injured right hand with his left, "drew a gun on me, and after I disarmed him, these others seemed prepared to do the same thing. My friends and I discouraged them, and then sent for you. Now we'd like to get out of here without any unfortunate accidents."

Sheriff Hitchcock looked at the young man and said, "Is this true, Gates?"

"This one said he was a friend of Rufus King's," Gates

105

replied, inclining his head towards Clint. "Those other two are friends of his, so they must be friends of King's, also."

"So you decided to kill them."

"Rufus King killed my father, Sheriff," Gates reminded the lawman.

"I was there, Gates," the sheriff reminded the kid. "Your father was a friend of mine, remember?"

"And you're gonna help them?" Gates asked.

"I'm going to help them get out of this saloon alive, if that's what you mean," Hitchcock said.

"Hitch, you can't—"

"Shut up!" the sheriff snapped. He looked at Clint and said, "You and your friend better wait for me outside. We'll talk at my office."

"Our pleasure, Sheriff," Clint said.

He and Hammer began to sidestep to the saloon entrance, and Dan Chow simply disappeared from the balcony, going back the way he had come.

Outside the three converged and holstered their guns.

"This is getting crazy," Hammer said. "We're threatened in one town because we're hunting King, and threatened in another because they think we're his friends."

"At least we know he isn't welcome in every town in Nevada," Clint said.

"That helps a lot," Hammer said, "considering we don't know which town is which."

Sheriff Hitchcock came out of the saloon and, walking past them without pausing said, "Come to my office."

"Shall we go to his office?" Clint asked.

"Seeing as how he asked so nice," Hammer said, "I think we should."

They followed the sheriff to his office and waited until he had seated his bulk behind his desk.

"You fellas want to tell me who you are?" he demanded,

glaring at them from beneath bushy, steel-gray eyebrows. "I know you ain't friends of Rufus King."

"How do you know that?" Hammer asked.

Hitchcock looked directly at Hammer and said, "Rufus King hates blacks, for one thing."

"You got that right."

"And I'd be willing to bet he feels the same way about Chinamen," the sheriff added, looking at Dan Chow.

"What about white men?" Clint asked.

Hitchcock looked at Clint, and then impressed him by saying, "You're Clint Adams, aren't you?"

"That's right."

"I thought I recognized you," the lawman said. "I saw you once, years ago when you still wore a badge. Rufus King would never be friends with even an *ex*-lawman."

"All right, Sheriff," Clint said. "We're not friends of his, but we are looking for him."

"Why claim that you're friends?"

"Because we've almost gotten killed a couple of times by people who were friends of his," Hammer said.

"Or who were just afraid of him," Clint added.

"Well, there's enough of each in this territory," Hitchcock said, "although how he got so many friends is beyond me. He's a mean, vicious, cold-blooded killer."

"We are aware of that," Dan Chow said.

Hitchcock glanced at Dan Chow, then looked at the Gunsmith again and said, "You a bounty hunter now? I hadn't heard that about you."

"No, I'm not a bounty hunter," Clint said.

"Neither are we," Hammer said, "if you care."

"Why are you looking for King, then?"

"We each have a personal score to settle with him," Clint said. "We happened to cross paths, and decided to join forces."

"Well, you should have brought a few more forces with you," Hitchcock said, "because if you find King, you're going to find a lot more than you bargained for."

"We understand he has quite a large family," Dan Chow said.

" 'Family' is not quite the word for it," Hitchcock said.

"What do you mean?"

"Well, he's got a couple of brothers, and some cousins, but other than that the rest of his family is not really related to him. People have just come to call the gang the King family."

"Well known, are they?" Hammer asked.

"In Nevada, yes," Hitchcock said. "They rarely seem to operate as a group in other areas, however, so outside of Nevada no one seems to have heard of them."

"We're taking him on on his own home ground, then," Clint said.

"Exactly," the lawman said, "and I don't envy you the task."

"You seem to know a lot about them," Hammer said.

"I know all about them," Hitchcock said. "I know everything about them except one thing."

"What's that?"

"How to stop them."

"What's their specialty?" Clint asked.

"Banks, mostly," the sheriff said, "but they've hit their share of trains and payrolls."

"How long have they been operating?" Hammer asked.

"Years," Hitchcock said. "It all started with their father, Ralph, and his brother, Rupert."

"Who's the leader of the gang now?" Clint asked. "Is it Rufus King?"

"No," Hitchcock said. "Rufus is the youngest brother, and he's the wanderer. He prefers to travel around, taking advantage of his family's reputation. He's been known to terrorize whole towns that way.''

''A whole town terrorized by one man?'' Hammer asked.

''They're afraid of him,'' the sheriff said, ''or rather, of what his gang would do to the town if they didn't treat him right.''

''That's crazy,'' Hammer said.

''I won't argue with you on that count,'' Hitchcock said.

''Can you give us any kind of a hint as to where we can look for him?'' Clint asked.

''If I knew that, Adams,'' Hitchcock said, ''I'd be out there with a posse. They've hit the bank in this town twice, and have killed three people in the process.''

''That boy's father?'' Hammer said.

''He was one of them, yes,'' Hitchcock said.

''How many men does he have in this—this family of his?'' Clint asked.

''Twenty,'' the lawman said. ''Maybe more.''

''How can twenty men be invisible, Sheriff?'' Hammer asked.

''I don't know,'' Hitchcock answered. ''There's got to be a hole somewhere out there where they're hiding.''

''Well,'' Hammer said, ''we're gonna have to find that hole and plug it up.''

''Just the three of you?''

''Unless you wish to come along,'' Dan Chow said, ''three shall have to be enough.''

Hammer and Dan Chow moved towards the door to leave, but Clint had a couple more questions before he was ready to go.

''Is King's father dead, Sheriff?''

''Not that I know of.''

''Is he with them?'' Clint asked. ''The gang, I mean?''

''I don't know,'' the lawman said. ''He'd be an old man

now. Pretty near seventy, I guess.''

"No other family?''

"Rufus, and his older brother, Reese—he's the leader—
oh yeah, they have a sister, too, younger than Rufus.''

"A father and a sister,'' Clint said. "If we can find
them—where were the Kings born?''

"Right here in Nevada,'' Hitchcock said. "A town called
Kingdom.''

"Kingdom?'' Clint asked.

"Now that figures,'' Hammer said from the door.

"Can you point us in the right direction?'' Clint asked.

Hitchcock gave them directions to Kingdom, and then told
them he wouldn't advise that they go there.

"Why not?'' Hammer asked.

"There's not much left of that town,'' the sheriff said,
"not since the Kings moved on.''

"Ghost town?'' Clint asked.

"Might as well be,'' Hitchcock said.

"Well, thanks for the information, Sheriff,'' Clint said.

"Are you going to be staying around here very long?''
Hitchcock asked in his best lawman voice.

"I'm not sure,'' Clint said. "We'll have to let you know.''

"I'd appreciate it if you would,'' Hitchcock said. "I'd like
to be ready if there's going to be more trouble.''

The three men left the sheriff's office and talked on the
boardwalk out front.

"What now?'' Hammer asked. "Head for Kingdom?''

"The horses need rest,'' Clint said, "and one or two of us
do too, I'd bet.''

Hammer and Dan Chow looked at one another, but neither
of them said a word.

"We'll get started in the morning,'' Clint said. "At least
now we have a destination in mind.''

"Yeah," Hammer said, "Kingdom—only I hope we don't end up finding Kingdom Come."

While Hammer and Dan Chow went to the hotel to get three rooms, Clint went back into the sheriff's office to let Hitchcock know that they were staying overnight.

"You think that's smart?" Hitchcock asked.

"We're pretty worn out, Sheriff," Clint said, "and so are our animals. I wouldn't worry too much if I were you. We'll be out of your town by morning."

"The morning is not what I'm worried about," Hitchcock said. He stood up, a big, shaggy, overweight man in his early sixties who still took his job very seriously, even after thirty years of wearing a badge.

"All right," he sighed, scratching his head, "I'll keep my ears open tonight. Young Gates and some of his friends might want to try you and your friends again while you're asleep."

"Appreciate it, Sheriff," Clint said.

"Adams . . ." Hitchcock said.

"Yeah?"

"You're an ex-lawman, so I'll count on you to keep your two friends in line."

"Don't worry, Sheriff," Clint said. "My friends and I are not looking for trouble—at least, not in your town."

"Well, I've learned over the years that trouble rides a fast horse, friend," Hitchcock said. "Sometimes it's just impossible to outrun."

TWENTY-FIVE

The hotel had two floors of rooms above the lobby floor, and they succeeded in getting three rooms on the top floor. Hammer and Clint had rooms right next to one another; Dan's was at the end of the hall.

"How are we going to work this?" Hammer asked.

"I guess one of us will have to stay awake at all times," Clint said. "We'll stand watch, just as we did on the trail. Whoever is awake will just have to keep his door open."

"That's fine," Hammer said, "but I for one am not ready to turn in yet."

"Want to go out and look for some trouble?" Clint asked.

"Only if it comes in a skirt," the black man said. "Or a big glass."

"Okay, I get the picture, but maybe I'll go along just to be on the safe side."

"I will stay in my room," Dan Chow said.

"Will you be all right alone?"

"I have had much practice being alone," Dan Chow said. "I will be fine."

"All right," Clint told Hammer. "Let's leave our gear in the rooms and get going."

Clint left his saddlebags and rifle in his room and went back out into the hall at the same time Hammer did.

"Ready?" he asked.

"Do you think that little Chinaman is going to be okay by himself?" Hammer asked.

"I think that little Chinaman is more okay alone than either one of us would be," Clint said. "Let's go."

When they got outside it was just getting dark and Clint said, "I don't think we should go back to the same saloon."

"That's fine with me," Hammer said. "I didn't see no good-looking women there, anyway."

"I guess we can just walk around and find another one, then," Clint said.

"Or maybe a whorehouse," Hammer said. "I ain't exactly particular at this point. I never got a chance to finish what I started with that redhead."

"You did seem to be a little unfulfilled when we broke in," Clint said, grinning.

"Yeah, well I aim to *get* fulfilled, and do some fulfilling before we leave this town. I tend to get a little testy when I ain't had a woman for a long time."

"Is that so?" Clint said. "I don't know that I'd be able to tell the difference."

"You just ain't known me long enough, is all," Hammer said. "After I've had some female companionship I get to be downright likable."

"That I'd have to see to believe," Clint said. Hammer gave him a hard look and they went in search of another saloon.

TWENTY-SIX

Clint and Hammer had no trouble finding another saloon, and quickly installed themselves at a corner table with a beer in front of each of them. Once again, Hammer drew attention, but since the two men were sitting quietly at a table, the attention gradually decreased.

There were a couple of girls working the saloon, but they didn't appeal to either man.

"I've seen better looking dogs," Hammer said, his distaste showing on his face.

"I guess I have to wait a little longer for you to become likable, huh?"

"When I finish this beer, I'm going hunting for something better than these, Clint," Hammer said. "You're welcome to join me if you like."

"I'm with you short of paying for it," Clint said. "I don't pay for my pleasure."

"It don't matter to me one way or the other," Hammer said. "At least if you pay for it you know that all the gal has on her mind is earning her money and keeping you happy."

"I guess that's one way to look at it," Clint replied.

The Gunsmith realized that he was not among the major-

114

ity, being a man who liked to give pleasure during sex as well as receive it.

Hammer, he suspected, was the more typical western male, concerned with his own wants and needs when it came to sex. Clint Adams had much too much respect for women to treat them any other way than what he was used to. And he could not respect a woman who was having sex with him just for money.

As they were finishing their beers a man walked into the saloon, saw them in the corner, and then quickly backed out.

"Did you see that?" Clint asked.

"Yeah, I saw it."

"Recognize him?"

"No, I didn't get that good a look."

"I did," Clint said. "He was in the saloon when the Gates kid pulled his gun."

"Uh-huh," Hammer said. "That brings up a few interesting questions."

"Like is he waiting outside right now for us to come out?" Clint offered.

"Exactly."

"Maybe he just backed out, looking to avoid trouble," Clint suggested.

"Yeah, maybe," Hammer said.

They exchanged glances and then Hammer said. "I'll go out the back."

"What if there is no back door?"

Hammer stood up, towering over everyone else in the place, and said, "I'll make one."

"Five minutes," Clint said, and Hammer nodded.

Clint swirled the dregs of his beer around the bottom of his glass for five minutes, then pushed his chair away from the table and stood up. He attracted very little attention walking to the batwing doors, and he hoped that would be true after he went through them.

As he eased himself through the batwing doors and onto the boardwalk, the only person he could see was Hammer, who was coming out of the alley next to the saloon.

"Anything?" Clint asked.

Hammer eased the hammer of his drawn weapon down and said, "Nothing. I think maybe we're jumping at shadows."

"Can't blame us for that," Clint said. "First shadow we don't jump at could put a bullet into us."

"You got that right," Hammer said, holstering his gun.

"Still . . ."

"Still what?"

"It bothers me the way he backed out so quick," Clint said. "Like he couldn't wait to go and tell somebody that he saw us."

"But not all of us," Hammer said.

"You're right," Clint replied. "He saw two of us and hurried out—"

"—to tell somebody that one of us was alone," Hammer finished for him.

They started walking quickly towards the hotel, and it was when they were halfway there that they heard the shots.

"Let's go!" Clint shouted, but Hammer was already a step ahead of him, gun in hand.

They charged through the front door of the hotel and saw the clerk staring up the stairs.

"Where?" Clint began to ask, but just then they heard a second shot, and then a third close on its heels.

"Upstairs," Hammer said, and he ran up the steps, followed by Clint, both fearing the worst.

Just before they entered the second floor hallway they

heard another shot, and as they rounded the corner they saw a man stagger out into the hallway from Dan Chow's room.

"Dan," Hammer shouted. They started down the hall towards the Oriental's room and suddenly two men burst through the door. When they spotted Hammer and Clint they turned to bring their weapons to bear and the two partners had no choice but to fire.

Clint shot the man on the right twice, and Hammer put two holes in the other man before either of them could fire a shot. They fell in a heap atop their fallen comrade.

Hammer leaped over the three men without pausing and burst into Dan Chow's room. Clint paused only long enough to determine that the three men were dead—the first from a *shuriken* in the throat—and then followed Hammer into the room.

"You damned Chinaman!" Hammer was saying as Clint entered.

The Gunsmith looked around the room and saw a fourth body at the base of the bed, and a fifth hanging in and out of the shattered window. Dan Chow, apparently unmarked, was standing by his bed, regarding his friends with a serene look on his face.

"I told you I was all right alone," he said.

Hammer turned to Clint and said, "These poor bastards didn't have a chance. They were outnumbered!"

TWENTY-SEVEN

Dan Chow's story to the sheriff was simple. Two men had come through the window, and at the same moment three had broken down the door. They fired at Dan Chow, who had then dispatched three of them—one with each *shuriken*—and the Chinese admitted that he was about to use his gun, as distasteful as the prospect was to him, when Clint and Hammer had come along and taken care of the last two men for him.

"Had they not," he finished, "I would have taken care of them, as well."

They were all in the sheriff's office and Hitchcock was seated behind his desk, shaking his head helplessly. "All five of these men were in the saloon this afternoon when Gates drew on you."

"Where's Gates?" Clint asked.

"I don't know. I've got my deputy out looking for him."

"Could that young man have that much influence on grown men?" Clint asked.

"His father was well liked," Hitchcock said. "If they thought they were avenging him, yes."

"Damn!" Clint said. "I hate senseless killing, and that's

118

what this was. Didn't you tell Gates the story we told you, that we weren't friends of King?''

Hitchcock shook his head and said, ''I wasn't able to find him.''

''That's great,'' Hammer said, ''That kid can gather up a few more friends and try again.''

''Brought it on yourselves,'' Hitchcock said. ''You should have left town right away.''

''Wait a minute,'' Hammer said, standing up, ''just whose side are you on anyway, Sheriff?''

''Easy, Hammer—'' Clint said.

''I'm on my side, friend,'' Hitchcock said. ''You're disrupting my town by being here, you got five of my citizens killed. I ain't looking for anymore.''

''Well, we weren't looking for those five,'' Hammer said, ''but they chose to go after our friend here when they thought he was alone. They had a choice, Sheriff, and they made the wrong one. That ain't our fault.''

''Well, we look at it a little different then, don't we?'' Sheriff Hitchcock said.

''Yeah, I guess we do,'' Hammer said. He turned and stalked out of the office.

Dan Chow looked at the lawman with that serene look on his face, then turned away and walked out.

''My friends and I will spend the night, Sheriff,'' Clint said, ''and be gone in the morning.''

''Yeah,'' Hitchcock said, unhappily.

Clint turned and headed for the door, and as he reached it Hitchcock said, ''Adams.''

''Yeah?'' Clint asked, turning.

''Try not to kill anybody the rest of the night, hear?'' the lawman said.

● ● ●

They decided to spend the night in one room, with one man awake at all times, and when they left the hotel the next morning, Sheriff Hitchcock was watching them from in front of his office.

"You know," Hammer said on the way to the livery stable, "I think he'd probably lock us up if we decided to stay longer."

"He'd say it was for our own good, too," Clint said.

They saddled their horses, on the alert for trouble, since the liveryman had obviously decided not to be around that morning when they left.

"How'd the street look to you?" Hammer asked as they prepared to ride out.

"Normal," Clint said. "I think we just might make it out of this town without any more trouble."

"I think not," Dan Chow said, but didn't elaborate.

"Let's try it," Clint said, and they rode their horses out of the livery and down Main Street. As they passed the sheriff Clint nodded his head and touched his hat and drew no response from the lawman.

"Right friendly man," Hammer said.

They rode on a few yards further and suddenly a voice called out.

"Hold it right there!"

"Uh-oh," Clint said, reining Lance in.

"Shit," Hammer muttered.

They all turned their horses sideways to look behind them and saw the kid, Gates, standing in the middle of the street. His gun belt was turned around so that he could get at his weapon with his left hand.

"Can you believe this?" Hammer asked aloud. "This kid wants to draw on the Gunsmith with his odd hand."

"Take it easy, Hammer," Clint said.

"*I'm* taking it easy," the black man said, "but somebody

ought to give that kid the same advice.''

"Somebody will," Clint said. "Just sit tight, both of you."

"I'm gonna kill you!" Gates shouted.

"Which one of us you talking to, boy?" Clint asked.

That confused the boy for a moment, and he licked his dry lips. "Don't much matter to me none," he finally said. "You're all friends of Rufus King, and he killed my father."

"Well, while you're killing one of us, what do you think the other two are going to be doing?" Clint asked.

Again the kid had something to think about, and it didn't seem that thinking was his strong suit.

"Why don't you just go home?" Clint suggested. "Seems to me if you're going to kill someone you ought to at least wait until your gunhand heals up."

"You better go for your gun, mister," the kid shouted.

"If I do that, son, you won't live much longer," Clint said. "And if I don't kill you, he will," Clint added, pointing to Dan Chow, "or he will," he said, pointing to Hammer. "That doesn't seem to me to be something your father would have wanted."

"You're trying to confuse me," Gates said. "All I want to do is kill one of you. I don't much care what happens after that."

"Well, I do," Sheriff Hitchcock said. He had been walking up behind the kid while Clint was talking, and now he drew his own gun and hit the kid over the head with the butt end. The kid dropped his gun and slumped, and Hitchcock caught him under the arms before he could hit the ground.

"Much obliged, Sheriff," Clint said, "but I think I could have talked him out of it in a few more minutes."

"That's a few minutes more than I want you in my town," the sheriff said. "Turn your horses around and ride out, Adams, before this boy wakes up. I'd hate to have to hit him over the head again. Might end up killing him myself, that way . . . though Lord knows he's got a hard enough head.''

"Just keep him from coming after us, Sheriff," Clint said. "Maybe you can make him believe that we don't like Rufus King any more than he does."

"I'll talk to him," Hitchcock said.

"Good."

"Adams?"

"Sheriff?"

"You could have killed him fair, and you didn't," Hitchcock said. "His father was a good friend of mine. I—I appreciate it."

"Don't mention it, Sheriff," Clint said. "Don't mention it at all." He turned to Hammer and Dan Chow and said, "Let's go."

TWENTY-EIGHT

They had a rough idea where Kingdom was located, and the sheriff had given them two ways to go. They could ride through the next two or three towns until they reached it, or they could ride in a straight line over some rough country and cut some time off their trip. They camped that night and discussed it.

"If we bypass those towns in between we might miss King," Hammer said.

"Yeah, but on the other hand," Clint said, "he might be heading for Kingdom, and we'd be there ahead of him."

"What makes you think he's heading for Kingdom?" Hammer asked. "You heard the sheriff say it was nothing but a ghost town."

"That'd be a perfect place for a gang to hole up between jobs," Clint said. "Besides, Rufus King seems to be some kind of family man. He's got a father and a sister. Suppose they're in Kingdom, too?"

"And the sheriff knows it, you mean?" Hammer asked.

"That's a possibility," Clint said. "Maybe he works for the Kings, or maybe he's just trying to keep us from getting killed by bucking the whole gang."

"That's another reason we should go town to town," Hammer said. "We could catch up to King before he reaches his gang."

"And we could run into more trouble," Clint said. "We keep going town to town, we aren't going to always be so lucky."

Hammer looked at Dan Chow and said, "You're awfully quiet. This concerns you, too. What do you say?"

"I have said from the beginning that I would be guided by Clint in such matters," Dan Chow said. "I think we should go to Kingdom. We can stop just outside and see what the situation looks like."

"Right," Clint said, looking at Hammer. "This is a democracy, Hammer. What do you say?"

"I say I should have met up with the two of you before you brainwashed this damned Chinaman," Hammer said. He looked at each of them in turn and then said, "We'll go to Kingdom."

During Clint's watch Hammer came over to the fire and shook the coffee pot.

"Just made it fresh," Clint told him. The black man nodded, poured himself a cup, then sat opposite the Gunsmith. They didn't speak for a while, and then it was the black man who broke the silence.

"You sure ain't nothing like I'd have expected you to be," he said.

"I've heard that before," Clint said. "When did you decide that?"

"Wasn't hard," Hammer said. "You left that kid alive in Cord, and then you didn't draw on this kid in Albano."

"You got a rep, Hammer?"

"In some places," the black man admitted.

"Are you anything like your rep says you are?"

"Well, now," Hammer said, "I guess couldn't nobody be as bad as that."

"See?" Clint said.

"See what?"

"Even you exaggerate, and you're talking about yourself," Clint said.

Hammer gave Clint a hard look, then changed it to a wry grin and said, "I see what you mean. You know, there's a town where they say I killed seven men with six shots, raped six white women in one night, and ate a white baby?"

"And?"

Hammer gave Clint a reproachful look and said, "I ain't never ate a baby of any color."

The ride to Kingdom took several uneventful days, for which the three of them were very grateful. Sheriff Hitchcock's directions were remarkably good—perhaps too good. A blind man could have followed them, and that nagged at the back of Clint Adams's mind.

"What now?" Hammer asked as they looked down at Kingdom from the top of a rise.

"First we've got to find out if Rufus King is down there," Clint said.

"It doesn't look like anyone is down there," Hammer said. "The town looks dead."

"Not if you look closely enough," Dan Chow said.

"What do you mean, eagle eye?" Hammer asked.

"That house at the far end of town," Dan Chow said. "There is an article of clothing on a clothesline, which appears to be a woman's . . . undergarment."

"I see it," Clint said. "There's also a small garden alongside the house."

"A well-tended garden," Dan Chow said.

"You guys . . ." Hammer said in disgust, and then he

noticed something as well. "Hey, there's some smoke coming out of the chimney, too."

"Yeah," Clint said. "This town is not quite as dead as it appears to be."

"Yeah," Hammer said, "but who's down there?"

"Well, there's only one way to find out," Clint said. "You guys better make camp up here."

"You plan on going down there alone?" Hammer asked, pointing towards the little town.

"I'm still the least noticeable of the three of us," Clint reasoned.

"King knows we're on his trail," Hammer reminded him.

"So a white man rides into town," Clint said. "In case you haven't noticed, there are a lot of white men riding around out here in the West."

"Okay, so what's the plan?"

"I'll just ride on down there and see if he's there," Clint said. "Just a drifter riding into town looking for a drink and a place to rest."

"And if he kills you on sight?" Dan Chow asked.

Clint looked at them and said, "Well, then you'll know he's there, won't you?"

TWENTY-NINE

Clint guided Lance down the deserted main street of King-dom, Nevada and wondered how the place had looked years ago, before everyone had left. It just might have been a nice little town, and if that were the case it was ironic that such a town would have spawned a family like the Kings.

Not wanting to seem suspicious Clint simply did what he normally would have done upon entering a town. He pulled Lance to a stop outside the saloon and dismounted. He walked into the saloon prepared to find it empty, and was surprised.

There was an old man standing behind the counter, and when he saw the Gunsmith he started to laugh, a strange, high-pitched cackling sound that grated on Clint's ears.

Clint approached the bar and the man continued to chuckle, keeping a watchful eye on Clint.

"I thought this town was deserted," Clint said.

"Is," the old man said.

"You're here," Clint said.

"I've always been here," the man replied.

"Have you got any beer?"

"Nope."

"Whiskey?"

"Some."

"Can I have some?"

"You got money?"

"Yes."

"Then you can have some."

The old man took a dusty bottle off the shelf behind him, took out a glass and poured Clint a shot.

"That'll cut the dust," the old man said.

"Looks like you could use something around here to cut the dust, too," Clint said.

"I like it like this," the old man said. "This town is old, like me."

"You look pretty well preserved," Clint said.

The man had been big once; now he was simply tall and emaciated. His eyes had sunk into his head and he had very few teeth left. He looked to be eighty if he was a day.

"I take care of myself," the old man said, following it with a high-pitched cackle.

"And the town?"

"I take care of Kingdom, too."

"Alone?" Clint asked. "You take care of this whole town by yourself?"

"It's a small town," the man said.

"There's no one else here with you?"

"Do you see anyone?"

"No, but then I haven't been here long," Clint said. He decided not to mention any of the things he, Hammer and Dan Chow had seen from the rise.

"Are you going to stay?" he asked.

"Uh, I hadn't thought about it," Clint said.

"We have plenty of room at the hotel, you know," the old

man said. "Plenty of room, and the rates are very reasonable."

"Would I be able to get a meal?" Clint asked.

"Of course, of course," the man replied. "My daughter is an excellent cook."

"Your daughter?" Clint asked, remembering the laundry hanging behind the house.

"Yes," the old man said, cackling again.

"You said you were here alone."

"I didn't say that," the old man said, "you did. I said I take care of the town. My daughter, she takes care of me."

Clint had another drink while the old man went through another cackling fit.

"My little joke, mister," the old man said then. "Don't mind me."

"Is that it, then?" Clint asked.

"Is what it?"

"Just you and your daughter live here?"

"We have visitors from time to time," the old man said, "like you."

"Any other family?"

The old man stared at him for a long moment, as if he hadn't heard the question.

"You can go on up to the hotel and pick yourself out a room," the man said, finally. "I'll send my daughter over to cook you up something."

"Thanks," Clint said. He decided not to ask the old man any more questions right then. Maybe he'd be able to get something out of the daughter. "I'll see you later."

"Sure," the man said. "Come back for a drink after dinner."

"I'll do that."

Clint walked to the door, then looked back at the man before going through.

"Just down the street to the right," the old man said, and Clint waved and walked out.

"Don't forget to sign the register," the old man called after him.

THIRTY

Clint did not mount up outside the saloon, but walked Lance down the street towards the hotel. When he had the building spotted, he decided to keep walking until he found the livery stable. If he didn't unsaddle Lance and see to his needs, it might look suspicious. Also, he'd be able to check out the livery to see if there were any other horses.

When he reached the livery he found it empty, except for an old rig and an equally old team. The animals were so old that their bones seemed to stick out at odd angles. He thought that if they ever had to pull that rig with anyone in it, they'd probably drop dead.

He unsaddled Lance, brushed him and gave him some feed. Taking his rifle and saddlebags, he left the livery and headed back towards the hotel.

Suddenly he became aware of someone walking behind him, and turned to find a young girl approaching. She had to be the old man's daughter.

"Hello," she called out, breaking into a trot to catch up to him.

"Hi."

"You must be the guest," she said, smiling. Her face was very pretty, with a small, slightly pointed nose, wide-set brown eyes and a wide, thin-lipped mouth. Clint generally preferred full lips on a woman, but with this one it didn't seem to matter. Up close, she wasn't as young as he had first thought, maybe twenty-three or so, and she was almost as tall as he was. Her body was willowy, with small, high breasts and long legs.

"I'm the guest," he admitted.

"We don't get many people through here," she said. "I hope you won't mind talking for a while. I get tired of having nobody but Poppa to talk to."

"Your father said you'd feed me," Clint said. "You do that and we can talk all you want."

"Wonderful," she said, clapping her hands together glee-fully, like a little girl having a promise fulfilled.

Her hair was long, hanging down past her shoulders, and chestnut, and he enjoyed the way it swayed with her springy steps.

She led him to the hotel, chatting away happily about finally having someone to tell her the news of the world.

"Why don't you take room six," she said, hurrying behind the desk to hand him the key. "It overlooks the street and it's the best room in the hotel."

"Any chance of getting a bath?" he asked.

She stared at him a moment, then said, "We can talk about that after you eat."

"I don't suppose I could get some steak?"

"We've still got some venison that I shot a few days ago," she said, "and some fresh vegetables from our own garden."

"Sounds good," he said.

"It will be," she promised. "Get settled in your room and by the time you come down I'll have it on."

"Okay, thanks," he said.

He started up the steps and she called out, "What's your name?"

"Clint," he said.

"You wouldn't happen to have a newspaper with you, would you, Clint?" she asked. "It don't matter where it's from."

"I'll check my saddlebags," he promised. "Do I get to know your name?"

"Oh, of course," she said. "It's Erin."

"Pretty name," he said honestly. "I've never met a girl by that name."

"Well you have now," she said. "I sure hope you won't be disappointed."

As he watched her prance through the doorway into what was probably the dining room he thought that under better circumstances, he certainly wouldn't expect to be.

THIRTY-ONE

When Clint came down, the scent of venison and vegetables was in the air as promised. When he walked into the dining room all of the tables but one were covered with white cloths. On that one was a plate, a knife and fork, a glass and a bottle of whiskey.

"All I need now," he said aloud, seating himself at the table, "is some coffee."

"I'm just putting it on," Erin said as she entered the room carrying a basket of bread.

When she put it down on the table he could smell the freshness of it.

"Make it myself," she said proudly, reading the look on his face. "How do you like your coffee?"

"Strong, black and hot," he replied.

"That's what you'll get." She put a small plate of butter down next to the bread and said, "Get started on this and I'll bring your meal out."

"Thank you."

His stomach began to rumble as he breathed in the scent of the cooking meat, and briefly he felt a stab of guilt. Hammer and Dan Chow were probably feasting on beans and hardtack at that moment, but then he decided he deserved certain rewards for the risk he was taking. After that, there was no more guilt.

Just good eating.

After she had brought him everything but the coffee—which would come later—she sat down opposite him and said, "How about that newspaper?"

He took a folded paper out from inside his shirt and handed it to her. He hadn't even remembered putting it in his saddlebag, but there it had been.

"It's a couple of weeks old, and it's a small-town paper," he said, "but it's something."

"It's everything," she said, her eyes shining as she fondled it. "I haven't had something fresh to read in almost two months."

"Well, enjoy it."

"I will," she said, putting it aside, "later. Right now I want to enjoy you." He looked at her sharply and she added, "I want to talk to you—no, I want you to talk to me—no—" She stopped then and laughed. "I guess I don't rightfully know what I want, do I?"

"You'll decide," he said, "and I'll still be here."

"How's the meal?"

"It's delicious," he said, and she preened at the compliment. "You're one hell of a cook."

"One of my many talents," she said, but did not elaborate on the rest of them.

While he finished his meal he fielded questions from her, harmless questions about current events. By doing so he was building up credit with her. Pretty soon it would be his turn to ask them, and he could do so without suspicion.

"I'll get the coffee," she said when she saw that he was almost finished.

When she brought the pot back she said, "You finished it all."

"Nothing left over?"

"Leftovers go to waste," she said.

"How'd you know how much I'd eat?" he asked.

She smiled broadly and said, "Another one of my many talents, Clint. Looking at a hungry man and knowing just how hungry he really is."

"That's quite a talent," he said.

She poured him a cup of coffee and he tasted it and found it exactly to his specifications.

"Your talents impress me more and more, Erin," he said. "Where did you get a name like that?"

"It's Irish, I think," she said, "but that ain't why I got it. My ma and pa expected another boy, and were all set to name me Eric. When I came along, they just changed the c to an n."

"Clever."

She poured him another cup of coffee and then continued with her questions. Some of them he couldn't answer, like what were the young ladies wearing these days. He was not a very fashion-minded man, but she forgave him that.

When she poured out the last of the pot she said, "I'll clean up while you finish that."

"Can I help?"

"No need," she said. "I like doing it."

"Suit yourself," he said.

He poured himself another shot of whiskey and had it with the last of the coffee. Clint rarely smoked cigars, but after the meal he just had, one would have seemed appropriate.

"I thought you might like one of these," Erin said, approaching the table. She was holding out her hand to him and in it was a cigar.

"You are amazing," he said, taking it. "Is mind reading another one of your many talents?"

"I just try to make it a point to know what a man wants," she said.

"And do you know what I want?" he asked before he could stop himself. He hadn't meant it to sound so suggestive, but she either didn't notice, or chose not to show that she had.

"I think what you want right now more than anything else," she said, "is a bath."

"That's right," he said. "We were going to discuss that after I ate."

"Yes," she said.

"Where's the nearest tub?" he asked.

"Not here," she said. "There used to be one here but we moved it."

"To where?"

"The house at the end of town," she said.

"Your house?"

She nodded.

"Where I live with my father."

"You're offering me your own bathtub?"

"It's the only one in town," she said. "That is, if you don't mind using it."

"I don't mind," he said, "if you and your father don't mind."

"Poppa?" she said, laughing. "Poppa never uses it. I'm the only one who uses it . . . and now you."

"Well, then," he said, standing up, "lead me to it."

"Right this way," she said.

To while away the time, Hammer had been giving Dan Chow "black" lessons, as he had promised earlier. He tried to tell Dan just what it meant to be black. Dan told Hammer that he and the black man had much more in common than either of them had thought. "We've both endured much prejudice and hatred with dignity," Dan Chow told him.

Up on the rise Hammer watched Clint leave the hotel with the girl and chewed on his hard beef jerky.

"I wonder what he ate?" he asked Dan Chow.

They had assumed that Clint was eating in the hotel because of the smoke that had briefly risen from the chimney.

"It does not matter," the Oriental said. "It is his reward for the risk."

Hammer watched the girl as she led Clint to her house and said, "Hell, if I had known I'd find her down there, I would have taken the risk myself."

"Wait and see what happens when they reach the house before you make wish to change places," Dan Chow said.

They both watched intently as the girl and Clint reached the house and went inside.

"Nothing," Hammer said.

They waited awhile longer, and the girl came out the back of the house, walked to a well and began to bring water to the house.

"That son of a bitch," Hammer said, looking at Dan Chow, who simply shrugged. Hammer looked back down at the house and said, "That son of a bitch is taking a bath!"

THIRTY-TWO

Erin refused to allow Clint to help her with the buckets, and she filled the tub on her own while he waited.

"You might as well undress," she said at one point. "I've only got one more bucket to go."

He hesitated a moment and she laughed and said, "Go ahead and undress, Clint. I have two brothers. You don't have anything I haven't seen before."

"All right," he said.

He began to undress while she went for the last bucket. When she brought it in she poured it into the tub.

"I can heat a couple of buckets and add them in, which will make the water warm, but not hot. Is that all right?"

"That's fine," he said.

When she came back into the room with the first bucket of heated water he was already naked and in the tub. The water had been lukewarm to start with, so by the time she added the second bucket of heated water, the tub was warm.

That done, she stood next to the tub and began undoing the buttons on her dress.

"Erin—" he began, but she cut him off, speaking while she nonchalantly undressed.

"My father's too old to carry the water back and forth, Clint," she said. "You're a guest, and I'm too tired after doing it once."

She slid the dress from her shoulders and tossed it into a corner.

"I can't do it again," she said, "so I thought we'd share the bath. That is, if you don't mind."

"No," he said, staring at her lithe, nude body, "I don't mind at all."

She stepped gracefully into the tub, which was barely large enough for the two of them, and then stood there for him to examine.

Her breasts were small, but very firm, and her brown nipples were flat at the moment, but as he stared at them they began to harden perceptibly. The tangle of hair between her legs was already wet, and the sharp odor of her readiness permeated his nostrils. His erection slowly broke the surface of the water and rose out of it, like some sort of miniature sea monster.

Slowly she lowered herself to her knees, and he had to spread his legs so she could kneel between them. Her eyes were on the swollen head of his cock, and her breathing had become very rapid.

She leaned forward, putting one hand on either side of him, and pressed her body against his. With her eyes closed she rubbed her nipples against his chest, moaning deep in her throat, and the head of his cock began to rub against her pubic hair.

"Erin," he said in her ear.

"Mmm?" she replied dreamily, rubbing the lips of her cunt against his penis.

"How bad do you want this bath?"

"Not as bad as I want you," she said with her lips against his ear.

They rose together and stepped out of the tub. They dried

themselves and then she took his hand and led him through the house to the bedroom.

The bed was neatly made and while he watched her she turned it down.

Turning to him she asked, "You don't mind?"

"What?"

"Being used," she said, "to satisfy a need?"

"Would you have used any man who came along?"

"No," she said, shaking her head, "only one that appealed to me."

"Then why should I mind?" he asked.

He moved to her, took her in his arms and covered her mouth with his. Her mouth and body trembled and then her hunger overtook her. She thrust her tongue into his mouth and pressed against him so hard that they both tumbled to the bed, with her on top.

She moaned and groaned as they exchanged moist kisses, and then she began to kiss his chest and work her way down his body until she had her nose up against his cock.

"It's been a long time," she said.

"Are you sure you remember what to do?" he teased.

She smiled lasciviously and said, "Oh, I remember, Clint. That's one of my many talents."

He didn't know whether she meant sex, or a good memory, but in a moment it didn't matter. With a bob of her head she took him into her mouth and lovingly she began to suck, fondling his balls at the same time.

Christ, he thought, lifting his hips to the insistent suction of her mouth, *this girl does have talent*.

She moaned aloud with him in her mouth, squeezing his balls tenderly, and when she felt that he was just seconds away from release, she kept him from it.

"Ouch," he said, because it *had* been painful, but it was an exquisite pain.

"I'll fix it," she promised. She crawled on top of him

eagerly and fitted his large, swollen cock into her slick, hot pussy. "There," she said, settling down on him, "is that better?"

"Much," he said. He took the cheeks of her ass in his hand and then they were writhing together, banging their bodies into one another, again and again. Her cries were loud in his ears, but who was there to hear them but the old man, and Clint had no doubt that she'd instructed him to stay away.

"Oooh, my God, Clint," she moaned against his neck. Her open mouth began to glide over his neck and face, her tongue avidly licked his mouth. She bit his lips and his ears and scratched his chest and shoulders with her nails, and when he finally felt her body begin to tremble he gripped her tightly, because he knew that the passion that had been pent up inside her for so long would bounce them around the bed like an earthquake, and he didn't want them falling apart from each other at the wrong time.

When it came it was like two earthquakes trying to hold on to each other, but hold on they did, until she had used her insides to milk everything she could from him.

"A woman of many talents," he said in her ear.

She smiled and said, "I told you so."

THIRTY-THREE

"It's my turn," Clint said.

"For what?" she asked, rubbing her hand over his chest in circular motions. She snuggled up as close to him as she could get, enjoying the feel of a man again.

"To ask questions," he said.

"About what?" she asked, and her tone was guileless, which satisfied him.

"About anything," he said. "About what you're doing living in an empty town like this."

She laughed and asked, "How many towns have you ever had all to yourself?"

He laughed with her and admitted, "None."

"Walk into any store you want," she said. "Take any hotel room you want, any table in the dining room. Walk in and out of jail at will. Walk into the bank anytime you want."

"Any money in that bank?"

She laughed and kissed his right nipple, swirling her tongue around it until it was good and wet.

"No," she said, "but still we can walk in and out when we want." She blew on his wet nipple, giving him a chill.

"There's no more to it than that?" he asked.

She shrugged. ''I guess I just don't like being around a lot of people. Why, what did you think the answer would be?''

Clint shrugged and, choosing his words very carefully, said, ''I thought maybe you were waiting here for someone.''

''Waiting?'' she asked. ''For who?'' Was she trying to sound too guileless now, or was that just his imagination?

''I don't know,'' he said. ''A man, maybe.''

''You're the man I've been waiting for,'' she said, but her tone was light, betraying openly the fact that she didn't really mean it. It was also a way of evading the question.

''Sure,'' he said.

As he threw back the covers she asked, ''Where are you going?''

Pulling on his pants he said, ''I promised your father I'd have a drink with him, and then I think I ought to turn in.''

''You can come back here,'' she said.

''No, I think I'll go to my hotel room,'' he said. ''I don't want to put your father out.''

''He can sleep anywhere in town.''

''I'd rather he didn't have to do that on my account,'' Clint said.

She pouted, but stopped arguing. ''Will you be leaving tomorrow?''

''I haven't decided.''

''Do me a favor?''

''What?''

She got up on her knees so he could see her breasts and said, ''Give me a chance to change your mind?''

''All right,'' he said. He walked to the bed and kissed her on the mouth. ''And you know what?''

''What?''

''I'm sure it will only take one, too.''

He left the house and, as he had said he would do, headed for the saloon to have a drink with the old man.

He would have liked nothing better than to spend the night in bed with Erin, but that pleasure would have to wait for other circumstances—if it was still available to him then. He needed to be alone because when it got good and late—and dark—he was going to sneak out of town to fill Hammer and Dan Chow in on what was going on.

Right now he was going to have that drink with the old man, whose name he didn't know yet. Maybe the old geezer would be more talkative now that he knew Clint had slept with his daughter. In a way, that meant that he had Erin's seal of approval.

Then again, if Erin and the old man were who he thought they were, they wouldn't tell him much of anything about Rufus King, or the rest of the family. Not willingly, anyway; the old man just might be scatterbrained enough to let something slip.

Or maybe he wasn't scatterbrained at all.

When Clint walked into the saloon the old man was behind the bar, standing in just about the same position he had last seen him in.

When the other man spotted him he frowned and asked, "What are you doing wandering around town in the dark?"

"You invited me back for a drink, remember?" Clint asked. "Besides, it's not all that dark out." Clint had not paid any special attention to the fact that the streetlamps were lit, but now he realized that the old man must have lit them all himself.

"I thought you and my daughter sort of took a liking to each other," the old man said.

"We did."

"And you left her to come here and have a drink with me?" the man asked. He started cackling, and when he wound down to a chuckle he said, "You must want a drink pretty bad."

THIRTY-FOUR

"You got laid, didn't you?" Hammer asked, accusingly.

"That's not exactly the kind of welcome I expected," Clint said.

"What welcome?" Hammer asked. "While we're up here eating beef jerky and beans, you're down there having who knows what for dinner?"

"Venison."

"Venison!" Hammer said, looking at Dan Chow. Then he looked back at Clint and said, "And while we're up here freezing, you're down there in a warm bed with a hot woman."

"It's not cold up here," Clint said.

"You know what I mean."

"He also took the chance of being shot on sight," Dan Chow added.

"Was she worth it?" Hammer asked, grinning wickedly.

"I'll tell you about it another time," Clint lied.

"How many people are down there?" Dan Chow asked.

"Two," Clint said. "An old man and his daughter."

"King's father and sister, right?" Hammer asked.

"I didn't ask," Clint said. "The girl's name is Erin, and

146

the old man is just the old man. When I ask him his name, he just cackles.''

''Has he got an empty chamber or something?'' Hammer asked.

''More than one,'' Clint said, ''or none.''

''What's that mean?''

''Is there coffee?'' Clint asked.

''Yes,'' Dan Chow said.

Clint poured himself a cup of coffee and sat across the fire from Hammer and Dan Chow.

''Okay, so what did you mean by that?'' Hammer asked.

''I think he means that the old man is either crazy, or crazy like a fox.''

Hammer looked at both men in turn and then said, ''Can we not talk in riddles, here?''

''Maybe he just wants people to think he's crazy,'' Clint said.

''What people? You're the only one down there.''

''He probably acts like that whenever anyone comes to town.''

''Well, I think he's crazy for real,'' Hammer said. ''I mean, who else would walk down the main street of a dead town, lighting the streetlamps? Look at that town. It's like a whore who's all dressed up with nowhere to go.''

''Well put,'' Dan Chow said, and Hammer looked twice at the Oriental to make sure he was being complimented by the little man.

''All right, here's how it lays,'' Clint said. ''The only people I've seen are the old man and the girl. There's not even a hint of anyone else.''

''Then either King is on the way,'' Hammer said, ''or he's not coming.''

''Let's first work on the assumption that he's coming,'' Clint suggested.

"How long do we give that?" Hammer asked. "I mean, how long do we have to stay up here?"

"I think that you and Dan can ride into town tomorrow without arousing suspicion."

"How come?" Dan Chow asked.

"The girl was desperate for something to read, so I gave her an old newspaper," Clint said. "They don't know what's going on in the world."

"So?" Hammer asked.

"They won't have heard that there are three men—two of them very distinctive—who are hunting Rufus King."

"True," Hammer said. "So we can just hole up in the hotel. I'm sure there's plenty of rooms."

"The idea is good, but not the place," Clint said. "Pick out another building, one that really looks rundown. These people pretty much keep up any buildings they use, and so far that includes their house, the saloon and the hotel."

"Okay," Hammer said, "so we'll pick another place, where we can watch the street. As soon as King rides into town, we'll know it."

"All right," Clint said. "Now let's talk about what we'll do if he doesn't show up here in a day or so."

Hammer looked at Dan Chow, who looked at Clint, who looked back at Hammer.

"Let's not all talk at once," Clint suggested.

"The old man is here, and the girl is here," Dan Chow said. "There must be a reason."

"Such as?" Hammer asked.

"They're waiting for someone."

"Yeah, King," Hammer said.

"Possibly the whole gang," Dan Chow said.

"Yeah, possibly," the black man said.

"I think that they will definitely be here," Dan Chow said.

"Then you have a suggestion."

"If Rufus King does not show up within the next day or two, I will stay and wait. It will be up to the two of you what you want to do."

"You'd stay and wait for the entire gang to show up?" Hammer asked.

"When they show up, Rufus King will be with them," Dan Chow said. "Either that, or he will show up alone."

"Fine," Hammer said, "if King shows up first, you can kill him, but if the gang shows up ahead of him, you're in a bind, my friend."

"That will be my problem."

Hammer and Clint looked at each other over the fire, and then the black man said, "No, you damned Chinaman, it'll be *our* problem." He looked at Clint and said, "I'll be staying, too."

"I guess I will, too," Clint said.

"That's not really necessary," Dan Chow said.

"Oh, sure," Hammer said. "You'd like that, wouldn't you."

"What?" the Oriental asked.

"You'd like us to leave and start riding all over Nevada again looking for King while you sit here and wait for him to ride into your lap, so you can kill him. Well, my friend," Hammer said, leaning over and tapping Dan Chow on the knee, "I'm not going to give him to you that easy."

Clint studied Hammer's face as he was talking to Dan Chow, and he was amazed at how these two men had become friends, though he doubted that even they would admit it was true. Still, Hammer's real reason for staying was clear to Clint, just as his own reason was. Neither of them would leave Dan Chow behind to face the entire King gang alone.

Sure, Clint thought, *why let the man stay behind and commit suicide alone when we can all do it together? Isn't that the mark of true friendship?*

THIRTY-FIVE

Clint walked back to town in the dark, knowing that a couple of hours later Hammer and Dan Chow would be making the same trip while leading their horses. He hoped that Erin and the old man would have no occasion to go for a walk during the night.

When he reached the hotel he entered the same way he had left, through the back door. He had left it ajar, and found it just that way.

It was an odd feeling, ascending the stairs to go to his room in an otherwise totally empty hotel. His footsteps seemed to echo incredibly loud, and it made him wonder if the sound of Hammer and Dan Chow leading their horses would travel through the night to the other end of town. He hoped not.

Tomorrow had to be the day, he told himself as he walked down the hall to his room. King had to arrive then. They couldn't have been that far ahead of him, and in point of fact, it still bothered him that they had gotten to Kingdom first.

And if King was already in town, where could he be?

Clint stopped just short of his door as a thought struck him. Could King be bold enough to be hiding in one of the other vacant rooms? Had he watched Clint enter earlier that day, and was he simply waiting for Hammer and Dan Chow to

150

enter, as well? For what? So he could take the three of them on single-handed? That would be dumb. If King knew they were there, he certainly wouldn't try and handle them alone. And it would be impossible to hide an entire gang in a town that size.

No, the assumption they had to work on was that he wasn't there, and looking for a man who wasn't there was a waste of energy, and of time.

He put his hand on the doorknob to his room, and as he did he heard a sound. It could have been amplified by the stillness of the night and the emptiness of the town, but he doubted it. The sound had come from inside his room, the sound of a creaking floorboard.

He took his right hand away from the doorknob and placed it on the butt of his gun, then reached for and turned the doorknob with his left.

"Where have you been?" Erin asked when he pushed the door open. She was sitting up in his bed, naked to the waist, with the sheet and blanket covering her lower half.

Slowly, he stepped into the room and looked around, then took his hand away from his gun. He pushed the door shut, then turned to face Erin.

"I went out for a walk."

"You're a careful man, aren't you?"

"Usually."

"Why?"

"A man stays alive longer that way."

"There's only one kind of man who's that careful," she said, bringing her knees up and wrapping her arms around them. The move hid her breasts from his view, which was just as well.

"What kind of man is that?"

"A man on the run," she replied.

He didn't say anything.

"Are you on the run, Clint?"

"No."

"Then what are you doing here, in Kingdom?"

"Just happened to come across it," he said. "Looked like it was a nice little town once upon a time. Then I found out it had some pretty friendly people."

"What's your last name, Clint?"

"Don't tell me, let me guess," he said. "You're the sheriff of Kingdom, right?"

"Somebody's got to be, right?" she replied.

"What about your father?"

"Oh, he's the mayor."

"I see."

"Your last name?"

"I'll make a deal with you."

"What?"

"You tell me yours, and I'll tell you mine."

She smiled and said, "All right, but you go first."

"I thought ladies always went first," Clint said.

"Not in Kingdom."

She was icy now, and there was nothing of the little girl about her anymore.

"Adams," he said. "Clint Adams."

"I know that name," she said. "You've got quite a reputation with a gun." She frowned then and said, "I don't remember anything about you being wanted by the law. You used to be a lawman, didn't you?"

"Right."

"So you ain't running from the law," she said. "What are you running from—your rep?"

He didn't answer.

"Or maybe you're running *to* something," she went on, slowly. "Or maybe *after* something." She looked at him then and asked, "After some*body*?"

"Let's keep your part of the bargain," he said. "What's your last name?"

She lifted her chin and said, "King. Erin King."

"And your father?"

"You're after the gang, aren't you?" she asked.

"What gang?"

"You know," she said. "The King family, everybody calls them. Which one were you trailing?"

He didn't reply. He wanted her to keep talking.

"I'll bet it's Rufus," she said. Shaking her head she said, "Rufus is the hothead, the wanderer, the one who's always looking for trouble, and always looking for a new bed to sleep in." She looked at him then and said, "It is Rufus, isn't it?"

It didn't look like she was going to offer anything more on her own, so he said, "Yes."

"And you came after him alone?"

"Yes."

She put her thumbnail in her mouth and began to gnaw at it. Whatever was bothering her, he decided to let her work it out. He felt a break coming.

"You're not that dumb, Clint," she said. "You wouldn't take on the whole gang alone."

"I didn't know there was a gang," he said, "until I started tracking Rufus through Nevada."

"You must have found out soon after entering Nevada," she said. "You would have gotten help."

"I'm here alone, Erin," he said, holding his hands out from his sides. "You've seen that."

"Now look, Clint," she said. She was getting excited, and it had nothing to do with the fact that she was in his room with him, naked and in his bed. "This is important to me, so don't lie. You're not alone, are you?"

"Why is this so important to you?" he asked. "Because

you're part of the gang? Because you're worried about Rufus and the others?''

"I'm not—''

"Because your father is Ralph King, Rufus and Reese's father, and you're their sister?''

"What?'' she asked, looking shocked. "Clint, my father is not Ralph King. Old Ralph died last year.''

Clint frowned and said, "Then he's Rupert, your uncle.''

"He's not Rupert and he's not my uncle,'' she said. "Rupert died five years ago.''

"But you're Rufus's sister.''

She shook her head. "I'm not Rufus King's sister, Clint. I'm his wife.''

THIRTY-SIX

"His wife?"

"Yes."

"I didn't know he had a wife," Clint said. "I mean, I never heard anything about it."

"That's because he keeps me here," she said. "He goes off, robbing and catting around, and he expects me to be here when he gets back."

"And the old man?"

"He really is my father—Pete Falco," she said. "Rufe sent for him to keep me company."

"Is he really . . ."

"Daft? A little," she said. "He enjoys taking care of this town, though. Especially lighting all the lamps at night. He does that so that if the gang comes back during the night they'll be able to see."

"Then the gang does use this as a hideout?"

"Sometimes. There are times when two or three of them will come back, times when Reese and Rufe will come back. Every so often the whole gang shows up, and Poppa has a devil of a time cleaning up after them."

"You've got to cook for them?"

"Cook, darn and . . . and anything else they want from me," she said, lowering her head.

"He lets them use you?" Clint asked. "His own wife?"

She laughed without humor and said, "Sometimes they bring women back with them. Rufe doesn't spend any time with me, then, so I'm . . . available."

"Why do you stay?"

"We don't have any horses except for those in the livery," she said. "They can't go more than a half a mile or they'll drop dead."

"Walk, then."

"We can't," she said. "My father would never make it, and I can't leave without him. If Rufe came back and found me gone, he'd kill my father."

Clint stood there studying her, wondering how much, if any, of her story was true.

"Do you want to hear something terrible?" she asked.

"What?"

"I wake up every morning before my father and I go into his room to listen to him breathe," she said. "Lately, I've been hoping that he wouldn't be breathing. I've been waiting for him to die, because the day he does, I walk out of here."

She seemed sincere enough, but he still couldn't be sure.

"That's why I want to know if you came alone, Clint," she said.

"Why?"

"Because you're the Gunsmith," she answered. "If anyone can kill Rufe, you can, but even you can't take on the whole gang. If you had help, though, you could do it. You could free me."

She became agitated now, throwing the covers off of her so she could rise from the bed, heedless of her nakedness.

"Or you could take us away from here now," she said.

"On one horse?"

"You can't be here alone," she insisted.

"Whether I'm here alone or not, I can't leave, Erin," he said. "Not until I've settled with Rufus."

"What did he do now?"

"He tried to kill me, very nearly killed my horse," he said. "I set a lot of store by my horse."

"The white one?"

"No, this is just one I'm using while mine recovers," he said. "I want to find out why Rufus tried to kill me."

"I can tell you that," she said. "It ain't no secret that my husband's a fool."

"Why'd you marry him?"

"I grew up in Nevada," she explained, "hearing about the King family my whole life. When I met Rufus I thought he was . . . romantic. That lasted until after the wedding, when I found out what he was really like. By then it was too late. When I wanted to leave he wouldn't let me go."

She turned her back to him and strode across the room. He couldn't help admiring the dimples on her buttocks, and the way her hips swayed. He also couldn't help the way his body was responding to her.

"All right," she said, turning with her arms folded beneath her breasts.

"What?"

"I'll help you."

"How?"

"I don't know," she said, dropping her hands to her sides in exasperation. "Any way I can, but you got to promise that you'll take us away from here when it's over. Just to the next town, Clint. We can make our own way from there."

She stood there with her hands at her sides and her body tense, goosebumps covering her flesh. She couldn't have faked those.

"All right, Erin," he said. "All right."

Relief flooded through her and she ran to him and threw her arms around him.

"Oh, God," she said. "Thanks, Clint. Thanks."

"Take it easy," he said, taking hold of her arms.

He held her away from him and looked at her. She seemed to realize that she was naked and suddenly he could smell her again, that musky, ready odor of a woman who was eager to be taken.

Taking him by the hands she tugged him forward and said, "Come to bed, Clint. Come to bed and we'll close the bargain."

It seemed like an excellent way to seal a bargain, at that.

"Clint?" she asked later that night.

"Yes?"

"Will you kill him?"

He paused. "Do you want me to?"

"I thought I did," she said, "but now I know all I want to do is get away. If you have to kill him . . ." She let it hang there, and he didn't tell her that there were two other men itching to kill Rufus.

Still later Clint awoke and thought he heard something outside. Horses? Hammer and Dan Chow? He looked over at Erin, who was sleeping peacefully, and then closed his eyes and went back to sleep himself.

In the morning Clint asked Erin King one question. "When do you expect Rufus?"

"We never really expect him," she answered. "We don't have a calendar here, but I sort of keep my own. I call it my Rufus King calendar. See, if there's one thing I know about Rufe it's that he's real predictable."

"And what does this Rufus King calendar tell you?"

"He could have been here yesterday, might be here today," she said, "but he'll definitely be here by tomorrow."

"All right," Clint said. "Have you got the makings for a ham and egg breakfast?"

She grinned and said, "We've got chickens, but no ham. I can make some potatoes, though."

"That's fine."

"I'll get right to it," she said, and headed for the door.

"Erin."

"Yes, Clint?"

"Make enough for three," he said, and then went looking for Hammer and Dan Chow.

THIRTY-SEVEN

"Whooee!" Hammer was soaking up the last of his eggs with a fresh biscuit. "This gal can sure cook."

"That she can," Clint agreed.

Dan Chow didn't comment, but from the way he had eaten, he agreed.

Erin came out with a large pot of coffee, poured out three cups, and then went back into the kitchen without a word. Clint was surprised to see Dan Chow pick up his cup and take a sip.

"Shy, though, ain't she?" Hammer asked.

"She doesn't know what to make of you two," Clint explained. "You may be the first black man and the first Chinese she's ever seen . . . and Hammer?"

"Yeah?"

"You are one mean-looking son of a bitch."

Hammer laughed and said, "But likable."

"I'm still studying on that one."

Hammer picked up his cup, sipped it and said, "That's the best coffee I ever tasted. She do everything as good as she cooks, Clint?"

"I'll tell you about that another time," Clint lied.

"Yeah," Hammer said. "How are we gonna work this now, Clint?"

"Erin tells me she can just about predict when Rufus is going to come back," Clint said. "According to her, if he isn't here by tomorrow, he's not coming."

"That would mean he's dead," Hammer said.

"I do not like the sound of that," Dan Chow said.

"You want him dead, don't you?" Clint asked.

"No," Dan Chow said with cold eyes. "I want to kill him. There is a difference."

"There sure is."

"All right. We will work on the assumption that he's coming today or tomorrow."

"We don't know if he'll be alone, though," Hammer said.

"That's right," Clint agreed. "I think that the only safe assumption we can make as far as that goes is that he'll arrive with the whole gang."

"Be prepared for the worst," Dan Chow said.

"Exactly."

"How do you suggest we do that?" Hammer asked. "If they've got twenty men or more, we're bucking at least seven to one odds. That's not a good bet in any game."

"It's the only game we've got," Clint said, "we've just got to tilt the odds a little more our way."

"And you know just how to do that, don't you?" Hammer asked.

"I've got a few ideas."

"I thought you might. Is there anywhere around here we can get a drink? That old man open the saloon this early?"

"I expect he does."

"Well, why don't we go over there," Hammer suggested, standing up, "and you can tell us all about it."

Clint looked at Dan Chow, who nodded, and then said, "Let's go."

THIRTY-EIGHT

Clint laid it out in the saloon, with the old man listening and cackling away.

"He surely is minus a chamber or two, ain't he?" Hammer said at one point.

"He's harmless," Clint said.

"So what you're telling us," Hammer said, "is that we're gonna hold off twenty or more men just by being up on the rooftops and shooting down at them?" Hammer shook his head and added, "Seems to me somebody tried that on us not too long ago."

"Yeah," Clint reminded him, "but they were outnumbered."

"Oh," Hammer said, "*that's* what happened."

"Look," Clint said, getting serious, "we've got a wide open town here. We've got access to anything we want."

"Is there dynamite here?" Hammer asked.

"I don't know," Clint said. "We'd have to look and see. Have you handled dynamite before?"

"Once or twice."

"All right, why don't you go and look see what you can find?" Clint suggested. "If not dynamite, maybe there's some gunpowder handy."

"Whatever we find is liable to be old and unstable," Hammer warned.

"If it's all we've got it'll have to do."

"You got it," Hammer said. He knocked back his whiskey, stood up and left the saloon.

"He is a good man," Dan Chow said, and Clint looked at him in surprise.

"We're all good men, Dan," Clint said, "all three of us. But we're going to have to be better than good to get through this if the whole gang rides in."

"We will get through."

Clint looked at the little Oriental and said, "Those *shuriken* of yours won't be much good in a fight like this."

"I will use my gun, Clint," Dan Chow said, "have no fear."

"I don't," Clint said. "Not where that's concerned."

"What would you like me to do while Hammer is looking for explosives?"

"Why don't you see what you can find in the way of guns?" Clint said. "When the shooting starts we aren't going to have much time to reload."

Dan Chow nodded and stood up. "Anything in particular?"

"Just anything that won't blow up in our faces," Clint said. "Can you handle that?"

He was sorry he said that as soon as it was out of his mouth, but Dan Chow simply walked out of the saloon without saying a word.

Behind the bar, old Pete Falco was cackling steadily to himself.

"What do you say, Pete?" he asked. "Any dynamite in this town?"

"Some," the old man said. "Might not even be as old as you think."

"That means that the Kings bring some in from time to time?"

"From time to time."

"Well, that would be right helpful of them," Clint said, "wouldn't it?"

"It sure would," Pete said, and started cackling again. Clint figured that one of these days the old man was going to start cackling and not be able to stop.

THIRTY-NINE

"It's not much," Clint said, looking at the array of guns on the table. He had set himself in the jailhouse, breaking open the back door so that when the gang rode into town they wouldn't see the front open. Dan Chow had come in with an armload of guns and dropped them on the table.

"An old Springfield," Clint said, "a Henry, a Navy Colt, a Walker Colt . . ." Clint picked up the Springfield and said, "They all need cleaning. I can take care of that."

"Will they do?" Dan Chow asked.

"They'll have to," Clint said. "They'll shoot. I'll clean them so they don't seize up on us, check the firing pins . . . They'll have to do."

The back door opened then and Erin King came in carrying a gun case underneath her arm.

"What have you got there?" Clint asked.

She held it out to him and said, "It belongs to Rufus. I'm supposed to watch it for him. I'm giving it to you."

Clint opened the leather case and took out what was inside, handling it carefully.

"A Winchester seventy-three," he said.

"Rufe always thought it was something special," she

said. "He taught me how to clean it and care for it, in case he ever had to use it."

"You did a good job," he told her, running his hand along the barrel. "A real good job. Thanks, Erin."

"I told you I'd help you any way I could," she reminded him. She looked at the guns on the table and went to pick one up, but he trapped her hand beneath his on the table.

"Not that way," he said. "You've done enough."

"But—"

"You'll have to make sure your father stays inside, so he doesn't get hurt."

"All right."

"Why don't you start putting lunch together?"

"Sure."

As she went out the back door, Hammer came in past her. He paused to watch her leave, and then came in the rest of the way.

"What did you get?" Clint asked him.

"Some good stuff," Hammer said. "Dynamite, and not as old as I thought."

"Good. How much have we got?"

"Fifty, sixty sticks. They must have taken some with them the last time they left," he figured.

"They'll probably come riding in here fresh from a bank," Clint said.

"So?"

"So I had one idea," Clint said, "and now I've got another one."

"A better one?" Hammer asked.

"Maybe," Clint said. "I've got some checking to do with Erin, but it just may be."

Clint found Erin at the hotel, slicing up vegetables for lunch, and asked her questions, getting just the answers he wanted.

Now he knew he had a better way, one that might require less dynamite, less shooting, and maybe less killing.

How would Hammer and Dan Chow feel about that?

"It sounds good," Hammer said.

"Yes," Dan Chow agreed.

"We've just got to erase any sign that we were ever here," Clint said, "and then lie low. With any luck at all, we won't have to kill anyone."

"Except Rufus King," Hammer said, meeting Dan Chow's eye.

Clint had Hammer and Dan Chow replace the dynamite and guns, putting them back exactly where they had gotten them. Next, they picked out a structure which would be large enough to accommodate themselves and their horses.

"The horses will have to be comfortable," he explained, "if they make a sound, we'll be as good as dead."

"Right."

Once they had their hideaway picked out, they took turns up on a roof, keeping watch. Clint and Hammer were in the saloon when Dan Chow came down off the roof before his shift was up.

"They're coming," he said.

Clint and Hammer stood up and the black man asked, "How many?"

Dan Chow shrugged and said, "All of them."

FORTY

Twenty-two men rode into Kingdom, with Reese and Rufus King in front. Twenty of the men were on horseback, and there was one driving each of the two buckboards. One buckboard was loaded down with whiskey, and the other carried five women.

"Al, Dave, Fred," Reese King called out, "take the horses over to the livery. Mal, get the ladies settled in the hotel and then bring them to the saloon."

"Right."

"Rufe, you and I will put the money away," Reese said. "The rest of you get the whiskey put away. The party starts right away."

"All right," a couple of the men shouted, and everyone went about their appointed tasks.

Peering out through the spaces between the boards that covered the windows of the store they were in Hammer, Dan Chow and Clint Adams watched as the men and women dispersed.

"Shit," Hammer said.

"What?" Clint asked.

"I hope this ain't where they usually hide their money."

"Don't even think it."

"Right."

They watched all day as gradually everyone ended up in the saloon.

"How long do we wait?" Hammer asked impatiently.

"Listen," Clint said. "You can step right over there if you want to plug Rufus King. That is, if you don't mind getting shot all to hell right after."

"I'm just asking," Hammer muttered.

"Sooner or later some of the men will go over to the hotel with the women, according to Erin," Clint said. "The others will stay in the saloon and get good and drunk."

"Except for the two lookouts," Dan Chow said.

"Right," Hammer said. "One at each end of town."

"We'll take them out first," Clint said, "then the men in the hotel, and then the main force in the saloon."

"How many women did you count?" Hammer asked.

"Five," Clint said.

"That's five and two," Hammer said. "That makes seven, right?"

"Last time I looked," Clint said.

"That will leave fifteen in the saloon," Hammer said.

"These girls are pros, Hammer," Clint said. "Some of them are bound to take on two, maybe three men at one time. Let's just wait and see what develops, all right?"

"I was never much good at waiting in tight places," Hammer said.

"You should have told us that before," Clint said. "We would have let you practice."

"Shhh," Dan Chow said, and they all fell silent and continued to watch.

"Look," Hammer said hours later.

Clint and Dan Chow had been trying to catch some sleep and now they moved to the window alongside Hammer.

"It's the old man," Hammer said. "He's lighting the lamps."

"Good for him," Clint said. "We'll be able to see."

"Right."

"Where's Erin?" Clint asked.

"In the saloon."

"Anyone leave yet?"

"Not a one."

"Good," Clint said. "They're going to be good and drunk, as promised."

"Yeah," Hammer said. They listened to the racket that was emanating from the saloon and the black man said, "They're having a good time in there."

"Sounds like it," Clint said.

"I wonder how much they got?" Hammer asked. "And what bank they got it from?"

"That is not our affair," Dan Chow said.

"We just going to leave the money behind when we leave?"

"Let's make sure we do leave," Clint said, "before we start deciding what to take and what to leave behind."

"At last," they both heard Dan Chow say, and they were both surprised. It was the first time they had ever heard any real emotion betrayed by the Oriental's tone.

Four men had stepped from the saloon and with them were two of the women. They laughed and drank their way over to the hotel and disappeared inside.

"They look like they'll be in one room," Clint said.

"Never could stand having another man around while I was with a woman," Hammer said. "Now, another woman . . ."

"That makes six," Clint said, and they continued watching.

Ten minutes later two men and two women left the saloon and walked to the hotel—actually, they staggered, but they made it, and that was what was important.

"Ten," Hammer said.

"One woman left," Clint said.

"I hope she's a three-man woman," Hammer said, but she wasn't. When the final woman stepped from the saloon, she was accompanied by two men.

"That makes thirteen," Clint said, as they watched the couple disappear into the hotel.

"The Kings are still inside," Hammer said.

"You two better take care of those lookouts," Clint said. "I'll meet you behind the hotel."

"Right," Hammer said. "Let's go, Chinaman."

Hammer and Dan Chow left and Clint continued to watch until it was time to go. No other men had left the saloon during that time.

When Clint met Hammer and Dan Chow behind the hotel, he knew that the two lookouts were dead. His two partners wouldn't want to risk either man waking up, getting loose from bonds, and sounding an alarm.

"Done," Hammer said when he met Clint, and Dan Chow uttered the same word when he met them.

"Let's go in, then," Clint said. "Let's find out if that first group ended up in the same room. We'll take them first."

"Quietly," Hammer said.

"Of course," Clint said, "if you can keep those big feet from making too much of it."

"Let's go," Dan Chow said, and he actually sounded impatient and keyed up. The closer they got to Rufus King, the more he seemed to lose that serenity he'd displayed all along.

Clint pushed the back door open and they crept up the stairs, the big black man surprisingly light on his feet.

This was it, the Gunsmith thought, *this was going to be the end of it . . . finally!*

FORTY-ONE

They inched along the hallway and chose the room from which most of the noise was emanating. There were moans and groans and the sound of squeaking bed springs.

"This must be it," Clint said.

It was decided that Dan Chow and Clint would enter while Hammer watched the hall, just in case someone came out of one of the other rooms, or someone else came into the hotel.

Clint moved to one side of the door, and Dan Chow to the other. Clint would turn the knob, shove the door open, and Dan Chow would enter first.

Clint held up one hand, turned the knob with the other one, then dropped his hand in a chopping signal motion and pushed the door open.

Dan Chow leaped into the room and as Clint followed he heard a sigh and a strangled cry, like a scream cut off in someone's throat.

He cocked his gun and pointed it at the men in the room, who were clustered around one large bed. Dan Chow also had his gun out, and the men stared popeyed at the strangers.

"First man who makes a sound dies," Clint said in a whisper. "We don't want to interrupt anyone else's fun."

All of the men were naked and had full-grown erections,

but in the presence of the armed strangers, with death imminent, four erections rapidly shriveled away.

"Turn around," Clint told the men. They obeyed, and both Clint and Dan Chow stepped forward. Their guns rose and fell twice, and the men crumpled to the floor. Clint could see that one of the men Dan had hit had a broken neck. It was then that he noticed the women on the bed.

They were both dead, each lying in a pool of blood with a *shuriken* in their throats. One of them had a terrified look on her face, her wide, vacant eyes staring at him.

He turned angrily on Dan, who had rapidly tied the four men up.

"Women react from reflex," he said, "without any thought. They would have both screamed."

"I won't let you kill the others," Clint said.

"They will scream."

"You let me worry about that," Clint hissed. "You'll cover the hall."

The little Oriental looked as if he were going to argue, but then he shrugged and turned to leave the room.

Hammer saw that something was wrong between Clint and Dan Chow when they came out into the hall, but he didn't ask.

Clint made a "you and me" signal to the black man, who nodded that he understood.

They moved to the next door. From the sounds coming from inside all of the inhabitants were occupied.

Clint turned the knob carefully, opened the door and peeked inside.

One man was seated on the floor, leaning against the bed in a drunken stupor. The second man had the girl on the bed on her hands and knees and was plowing her from behind, and she was making quite a din. Figuring he could handle this alone, he motioned Hammer to wait and stepped into the room. He took three quick steps and struck the man on the bed on the head with his gun, and he fell forward, pinning the woman to the bed.

"Oh, Jess," she sighed, "ain't you gonna come?"

Clint stepped forward and whispered into her ear, "Not tonight, honey." She stiffened, but he laid the side of his iron against her head and her body relaxed. Clint stepped back and kicked the other man in the head, just to make sure he was out.

Stepping out into the hall he whispered to Dan Chow to go inside and tie them. The Oriental gave him a rebellious look, but moved to obey.

Clint then motioned to Hammer, and they moved down to the next door.

He put his mouth to the black man's ear and said, "Nine."

Hammer nodded and held up four fingers, indicating he knew how many were left.

Similar sounds were coming from the door they were in front of, and the last one in the hall. Clint and Hammer split up, each stepped into a room and dispatched the man and woman in their own way.

The Gunsmith left his alive.

They checked the rest of the rooms, just to be on the safe side, and found them empty.

"That's it," Hammer said.

"Yes," Clint said, eyeing Dan Chow.

"He is annoyed with me," Dan Chow explained, "because I killed the women."

Hammer looked at Clint, and said, "I killed the man, not the woman."

"They would have screamed," Dan Chow said, but his former conviction no longer seemed to be in his voice.

"Let's get over to the saloon," Clint said. "We'll do it like we planned."

"Right," Hammer said, and Dan Chow nodded.

Clint moved towards the batwing doors, careful lest someone choose that moment to come out. When he felt that Hammer and Dan Chow had time to get into place, he drew his gun. He reminded himself that there should be twelve men inside, and mentally reviewed the layout of the saloon. Then he drew his gun, and stepped inside.

Hammer drew his gun and slammed through the rear door. He shot the first man he saw, who stared at him in slack-jawed amazement. He was vaguely aware of Clint at the front door, firing, and Dan Chow above, but beyond that his attention was riveted on the men he was intent on killing.

Dan Chow stepped out onto the balcony and calmly began firing at the men below. He was the only one of the three who immediately noticed the absence of both Reese and Rufus King, as well as Erin King, but he did not respond to that fact until the shooting was over.

"Ten," Clint said, as he and Hammer stepped amid the human wreckage.

"Ten?" Hammer asked.

"The Kings are not here," Dan Chow said, coming down the steps.

"They had time to leave while we were at the hotel," Clint said. "Damn it!"

"We can go get them," Hammer said, ejecting the empties from his gun and reloading.

"They'll know we're coming, though," Clint said. "They couldn't help but hear this."

"Where would they be?"

Suddenly they became aware of a cackling sound and

turned to see old Pete Falco stand up from behind the bar.

"You got 'em all, yes you did," he said, "except the Kings."

"Where are they, Pete?" Clint asked.

"They left with Erin," the old man said. "I expect they went to the house."

"We'd better get over there, then," Clint said, "before they have a chance to get their bearings."

"You and Dan run on ahead," Hammer said, "I'll be along directly."

"What's the matter?" Clint asked, and it was only then that he saw the blood.

"One of them sons of bitches got off a lucky shot, damn it," Hammer said. "I got a slug in my right thigh." The black man looked at Dan Chow and said, "Put a slug in him for me, Chinaman."

FORTY-TWO

Clint and Dan Chow ran the length of the town as fast as they could and as the King house came into view they saw that it was dark.

"Ease up," Clint said, grabbing Dan Chow's arm. "There are no lights."

"I will go around back," Dan Chow said, and before Clint could comment he was gone. He had no choice but to wait until he thought the Oriental was in position before making a move.

"Rufus King!" he shouted. "Are you in there?"

Silence.

"King, this is Clint Adams, the man you been bragging that you killed!"

Silence, but when Clint was about to speak again, Rufus King called out, "Son of a bitch, you're dead!"

"Not quite, King," Clint replied, "but your men are. It's just you and your brother now. Step out here and let's finish it."

"Go to hell!" another voice called out, which Clint assumed was Reese King.

"Reese," Clint called. "Send your brother out. We've got no beef with you, only him."

"Can't do that, Adams," Reese King replied. "He's a fool, but he's my brother. If you want him, you'll have to come and take me, too."

"If that's the way you want it."

Clint heard someone behind him and turned to see Hammer, dragging his right leg, coming up the street.

"You should have stayed put," Clint said.

"Ah," Hammer said, "I plugged the hole. It won't bleed for a while. What do we have?"

Clint told him the situation and Hammer said, "The girl's in there too, huh?"

"I assume so."

"I guess that means you don't want to rush the house."

"She might get hurt."

"She might be dead already, friend," Hammer said.

Clint paused a moment, then said, "You're right."

"Let's just set 'er on fire and see what comes running out," Hammer suggested.

"I wish I knew what Dan was going to do," Clint said.

"You've known that all along," Hammer said. "He's gonna kill Rufus King, one way or another."

"Yeah."

"Look!" Hammer hissed, and Clint looked up on the roof of the house. Dan Chow was there, carrying a lit torch.

"That damned Chinaman," Hammer said, with something close to awe in his voice.

As they watched Dan Chow moved to the four corners of the roof, setting each one on fire. The flames quickly moved down to the walls, and in moments the house was ablaze.

"That Chinaman is still up there," Hammer said.

"He's going to burn to a crisp."

As the house turned into a ball of flame they watched and waited for something to happen. They could no longer see Dan Chow and assumed that he had been forced to jump down and was probably covering the back again.

And then Hammer said, "Look."

The front door of the house opened and someone stepped out.

"It's the girl," Hammer said. "They're using her as a shield."

"Don't shoot," Clint said. "You might hit her."

Both King brothers were trying to hide behind Erin, searching the darkness for someone to shoot at. They themselves seemed to be standing in broad daylight as the flames lit the night.

"We've got to shoot," Hammer said.

"All right."

"I'll take Rufus."

"Which is he?" Clint asked.

Hammer looked and said, "I'll be damned if I know. They look alike."

"Take your pick," Clint said, and stood up. As he did he noticed that the front wall of the house was starting to fall forward.

"Erin!" he shouted desperately. "Run!"

The King brothers heard his warning and instinctively turned to look behind them. Erin broke free and ran and was clear when the blazing wall fell on the two brothers.

It took some time for the flames to die down. Dan Chow waited patiently while Clint and Erin tended to Hammer's wound. The Oriental seemed to feel cheated as he stared at the dying flames.

"He's hoping King will still be alive," Hammer said, shaking his head.

"He can't be," Erin said.

But he was.

•   •   •

When they all approached the steaming embers, they were shocked to see movement.

"My God," Erin said.

One of the charred bodies lifted his arm and reached towards them beseechingly.

Erin King stared at the body closely, and although it was barely recognizable, she said, "My God, that's Rufe."

Dan Chow moved quickly, stepping in among the smoking embers and straddling the blackened, charred body that was once Rufus King. He took out his gun and pointed it at the pathetic thing's head.

And then it spoke.

"Kill me," Rufus King pleaded in a barely human voice. "Please . . . kill . . . me . . ."

They watched as Dan Chow cocked the hammer on his gun, hesitated, and then eased the hammer down.

"No," he said to Rufus King, and walked away, holstering the gun.

"After all that . . ." Clint said. He turned to Hammer and said, "Kill him."

Hammer looked at Clint calmly and said, "Let him suffer on his own."

Clint stared at Hammer, who started to walk away. Clint called to him but he kept on walking. "Why did you want him so bad?" Hammer stopped and slowly turned towards Clint. "He killed her . . . my baby. She was only three years old and he rode her down after one of his jobs," he answered solemnly. The Gunsmith finally realized why Hammer would rather let the man suffer and die in time rather than kill him and save him the agony.

The apparition that was once her husband called her name and Erin covered her ears with her fists and begged Clint, "For God's sake, kill him!"

Clint drew his gun and stepped forward. He placed the

barrel against the smoking head of Rufus King and pulled the trigger.

Holstering his gun he thought, *And I'll be goddamned if I didn't end up killing him myself, after all.*